"Don't tell."

She reeled back at the gravelly, unrecognizable voice that hissed over the machine. An icy chill instantly gripped her soul.

"You'd better not tell a soul or I promise I'll kill you."

The answering machine clicked off. Still she remained unmoving, staring at the phone that had suddenly become an instrument of evil.

Was the call a joke? She instantly dismissed the idea. She realized instinctively that nobody she knew would think that kind of thing funny.

Oh God, what did she know? What had she forgotten that was so important somebody would threaten to kill her to keep it a secret?

DESPERATE STRANGERS

New York Times Bestselling Author
CARLA CASSIDY

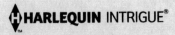

Recycling programs
for this product may
not exist in your area.

ISBN-13: 978-1-335-63910-3

Desperate Strangers

Copyright © 2018 by Carla Bracale

This edition published by arrangement with Harlequin Books S.A.

For questions and comments about the quality of this book, please contact us at CustomerService@Harlequin.com.

Printed in U.S.A.

Carla Cassidy is an award-winning, *New York Times* bestselling author who has written more than 120 novels for Harlequin. In 1995, she won Best Silhouette Romance from *RT Book Reviews* for *Anything for Danny*. In 1998, she won a Career Achievement Award for Best Innovative Series from *RT Book Reviews*. Carla believes the only thing better than curling up with a good book to read is sitting down at the computer with a good story to write.

Books by Carla Cassidy

Harlequin Intrigue

Desperate Strangers

Scene of the Crime

Scene of the Crime: Bridgewater, Texas
Scene of the Crime: Bachelor Moon
Scene of the Crime: Widow Creek
Scene of the Crime: Mystic Lake
Scene of the Crime: Black Creek
Scene of the Crime: Deadman's Bluff
Scene of the Crime: Return to Bachelor Moon
Scene of the Crime: Return to Mystic Lake
Scene of the Crime: Baton Rouge
Scene of the Crime: Killer Cove
Scene of the Crime: Who Killed Shelly Sinclair?
Scene of the Crime: Means and Motive

Visit the Author Profile page at Harlequin.com.

CAST OF CHARACTERS

Julie Peterson—Amnesia keeps her from remembering a deadly secret.

Nick Simon—A desperate man mired in grief who suddenly finds himself lying to the beautiful Julie in order to cover his tracks from a murder scene.

Tony Peterson—Julie's brother who has a secret of his own. Is the secret worth killing his sister over?

Joel Winters—Do his pleasant features hide a monster?

Max Peterson—Is it possible he wants the family business all to himself and he is willing to murder whoever stands in his way?

Chapter One

He wasn't a killer, but tonight he intended to become one. Nick Simon ran silently through the sultry July night. His heart beat faster than he imagined a meth head's pounded after one too many hits.

Not that he knew anything about drugs. In his thirty-three years he'd never even tried one. He'd always done the right thing. He paid his taxes on time, had never gotten a traffic ticket. He tried to be a good man, a thoughtful neighbor, and yet tonight he intended to murder a man he'd never met.

The flashlight, ski mask and gun in his pocket burned as if lit with the fires of hell. His thin latex gloves wrapped around his hands like alien skin.

At this time of night he hoped his victim was sound asleep. He hoped he didn't awaken to see Nick before he fired the gun.

Nick didn't want to see that kind of terror in anyone's eyes. But if anyone deserved to be terrorized and killed, it was Brian McDowell.

Nick slowed his pace when he was less than a block away from Brian's home. He tried to control the beat of his heart by taking in slow, measured breaths and releasing them equally slowly. Sweat tickled down the center of his back and wept down the sides of his face.

The night air was thick…oppressive, but it was dangerous to go in frantic. Frantic made mistakes and the last thing Nick wanted was to wind up in prison. A dog barked in the distance and he jumped closer to a stand of bushes.

At just after midnight on a Sunday this neighborhood had been quiet. There had been no traffic to hide from as he'd made his way the three blocks from where he'd parked his car.

Get in, get it done and get out. He pulled the ski mask from his pocket. He had his instructions and if he accomplished this kill, another man would murder Steven Winthrop… the person who had destroyed Nick's life.

For just a moment a wild, unbridled grief stabbed through him. Debbie… Debbie. His dead wife's name screamed in his head as visions of the last time he'd seen her flashed in his brain. Bloody…broken and gasping her last breaths. He mentally shook himself and just that quickly the grief transformed into a dark rage so great it nearly took him to the edge of madness.

He yanked on the ski mask and then withdrew the gun from his pocket. Justice. It was what he and five other men were looking for. Justice that had been denied. The six of them had forged an unholy alliance to make sure justice was finally served.

With the sickness and rage of loss still burning in his soul and ringing in his ears, he walked faster toward Brian's house.

The instructions he'd received along with the gun had indicated that Brian had to die between the hours of midnight and one, and that his house wasn't air-conditioned so entry could be easily made through an open window.

When he reached the red-brick ranch house, he skirted around the side. If he was going to change his mind about this, now was the time.

It wasn't too late for him to run back to his car and drive home without the bloodstains of another human being on his hands. But

Brian McDowell wasn't just any other man. He was a thief and a murderer. He'd beaten an old woman to death during a home invasion.

The cops had done their jobs. Brian had been arrested and charged with the murder when items belonging to Margaret Harrison had been found in his home. He'd been charged with the crimes and a year ago he'd stood trial. He'd been found not guilty when the evidence had mysteriously disappeared from the police department.

More important than anything Brian had done was the knowledge that if Nick killed Brian tonight, then somebody else would murder the man who had raped and killed Nick's wife.

With full conviction, Nick stepped around the side of the house and immediately saw the shattered glass of the sliding back door. A large red pottery planter lay smashed next to the door. What in the hell?

He approached closer, tension tightening his chest to the point of pain. He fumbled in his pocket for the flashlight. He clicked on the light and gasped.

Brian McDowell was just inside the door… on his back…with his throat slashed and what appeared to be a *V* carved into his forehead.

The blood was bright red, obscene vivid splashes of death on the white T-shirt the man wore. The coppery scent of blood hung in the air, half choking Nick.

He stumbled backward, bile rising up in the back of his throat. He swallowed several times against it as he turned first to the left then to the right to make sure he was still all alone in the dark. With trembling fingers, he yanked off the ski mask.

Run. The internal command held a frantic urgency and he immediately complied. He turned, ran back around the house and headed down the sidewalk in the direction he had come. His brain reeled with questions.

How? Who was responsible? Granted, Brian McDowell was a creep who any number of people might want dead. But what were the odds that somebody would kill him on this particular night, during this particular hour?

Who had gotten to Brian just a short time before him?

He couldn't help the edge of relief that fluttered through him. The man was dead and Nick hadn't had to pull the trigger. He wasn't even sure he would have been able to shoot him. Still, he needed to tell somebody, but the men had all agreed there would be no phone calls between them, nothing that could be easily traced.

He'd see them in a week's time when they all attended a meeting of the Northland Survivors Club. The place where they had all met a little over nine months ago.

Nick was two blocks from where he'd parked when a car without headlights came careering down the street. He froze and stared in horror as it crashed head-on into a large tree.

The car stopped running. The hiss of steam coming from the broken radiator was the only sound in the night. *Run*, that internal voice screamed. The last place he needed to be was down the street from a murder in the middle of the night with no reason to be there.

Run, that voice urged again. But he couldn't just walk away from the scene of the accident. Nobody had gotten out of the car yet, which meant somebody was probably hurt.

The airbag that had shot out with the crash depleted enough that one person was evident—a woman slumped over the steering wheel.

Even knowing he was putting himself in danger, there was no way Nick could just walk away. He yanked off his gloves and stuffed them into his pocket, and then hurried to the passenger door and pulled it open.

"Hello?" Her long dark hair hid her face. He knew better than to attempt to move her in any way.

Dear God, was she dead? He scooted onto the seat and picked up one of her lifeless hands. He quickly felt for a pulse. There... her pulse beat erratic and faint.

Crap, he didn't even have his cell phone to call for help and she needed medical attention as soon as possible. Noticing her purse on the seat between them, he quickly opened it and pulled out her cell phone.

He called 9-1-1, reported the address of the accident and that medical aid was needed. It was only after he disconnected from the call that a new panic set in.

If he hung around for help to arrive, then how was he going to explain his presence there? He'd done his duty, he'd made the call. Surely he could sneak off now.

He had one leg out of the car when she moaned. The pitiful mewling tugged at his heart and pulled him back into the car. "It's going to be all right," he said. "I've called for help."

She didn't move, nor did she moan again. Still he remained sitting next to her, bound to her by a whimper as he faced his own ruin.

He fumbled in her purse, withdrew her wallet and looked at her identification. Julie Peterson. She was thirty-one years old and lived less than a block away. An emergency contact listed her parents' phone number.

He stared at her driver's license picture for a long moment. Julie was a very attractive woman. He glanced at her left hand. No wedding ring. As the swirl of red and blue lights approached, a desperate plan formulated in his mind.

Although he wished her no ill-will, if she would just stay unconscious until they got her to the hospital, then Nick could establish an alibi. It was risky, but this whole night had been something out of a nightmare.

The next few minutes flew by as both a cop car and an ambulance arrived. The first order of business was getting the unconscious Julie Peterson out of the car and onto a stretcher.

Once the ambulance pulled away, Officer Tim Brown faced Nick. "You want to tell me what happened here tonight?" A tow truck pulled up where the ambulance had been.

The gun and ski mask in Nick's pocket

once again burned with sickly guilt. "Uh… Julie and I had an argument. She got angry and jumped into the car. I got in the passenger seat and, before I knew it, we'd hit the tree."

"I'm surprised you aren't hurt since your airbag didn't deploy," Officer Brown replied. Nick's stomach muscles clenched. Did the man suspect something wasn't right? A vision of Brian McDowell, bloody and dead, exploded in Nick's brain.

"Was there any alcohol involved here tonight?"

"No, none." He hoped like hell Julie Peterson wasn't a drunk.

"And specifically what is your relationship to Ms. Peterson?"

"Fiancé. I'm her fiancé." The words blurted out of him without thought of consequence. He just wanted to be allowed to leave.

"Can I see some identification?"

"I'm sorry, I don't have any on me. I ran out of the house to stop her and didn't think to grab my wallet."

"Your name?" The officer took down Nick's name and address, and then patted him on the back. "The tow truck will take care of the car and I'll get you to the hospital. I'm sure you're worried sick about her."

The hospital? His web of lies coalesced to form an imaginary noose around his neck. When Julie Peterson regained consciousness, all his lies could potentially result in a real noose around his neck for the murder of Brian McDowell.

The ride to North Kansas City Hospital took only fifteen minutes and, during that time, Officer Brown talked about the hot weather and how the humid, intense heat made people snap.

"Crime is always up during a heat wave like this," he said. "Thank God the weathermen are predicting a few cooler days next week." He shot Nick a quick glance. "You're a bit overdressed for July."

Once again Nick's heartbeat raced to a sickly pace as his brain struggled to make a rational response. "I have to wear warm clothes whenever I go to Julie's place. I swear that woman keeps her thermostat at fifty degrees during the summer."

Officer Brown chuckled. "My wife and I fight over the thermostat in our house all the time."

They parked at the hospital and, to Nick's dismay, Officer Brown accompanied him inside the emergency waiting area. "Julie Peterson was just brought in by ambulance," Officer Brown told the woman at the receptionist desk. "Please let her doctor know I've got her fiancé here with me."

"I appreciate your help," Nick said to him as he sank down into one of the chairs.

"It's my job." The officer sat in the chair next to Nick's.

Nick had hoped to shake the man and get out of there. Even though the cop had his name and address, he seriously doubted there would be any follow-up on the accident. But there would definitely be follow-up when Julie Peterson told everyone she didn't have a fiancé and she'd never seen Nick before in her life.

His stomach muscles twisted into a dozen painful knots as his mind displayed a horrifying picture of Brian McDowell. He'd scarcely had time to process that scene when the car crash had occurred.

And now he sat, next to a police officer, with a ski mask, gloves and a gun in his pocket that he'd intended to use for committing a murder. When Julie awakened and denied knowing him, would he be frisked?

The two men sat side-by-side for the next hour. Officer Brown made small talk and

Nick could only hope he responded as a worried fiancé, but he couldn't stop thinking about the gun in his pocket and the fact that he was seated next to a cop.

Finally a tall, balding doctor walked into the waiting room and headed for Nick and Officer Brown. They both stood, although Nick was sure Tim Brown's heart wasn't beating as frantically, as desperately, as Nick's. His wrists turned icy, as if feeling the cold bite of handcuffs around them.

"How is she?" Nick asked after the doctor introduced himself as Dr. Mitch Carlson.

"The good news is her physical injuries are relatively minor considering the circumstances. She has some bumps and bruises and a mild concussion," Dr. Carlson replied.

"Can I ask her a few questions?" Officer Brown asked.

Dr. Carlson frowned. "Now I'll tell you the bad news. She doesn't remember anything about the accident."

Nick held his breath. Hopefully, Brown would leave with this news and he could get out of there within minutes. God, he needed to escape.

"In fact," Dr. Carlson continued, "the last memory she has is of her birthday party ten months ago. She can't remember anything that happened between then and now. She's been moved to a room for observation." He turned to look at Nick. "I told her that her fiancé was here and she's asking to see you."

"I'll come with you," Officer Brown said. "I'd just like to follow up with her."

Dr. Carlson nodded. "I'll take you both to her room."

Nick followed the doctor and the police officer down a hallway with a sense of overwhelming dread. Was her strange amnesia real? Within seconds he'd find out. He'd either walk out of there with his lies intact or he'd be called out. With no good reason to be on the street where the accident had occurred, he'd eventually be tied to a murder he hadn't committed.

JULIE PETERSON WAS AFRAID. She'd been afraid since she'd opened her eyes in the ambulance with no idea of what had happened to her or where she was.

She'd been told she'd been in a car accident. The nurse had explained to her that her car had hit a tree. But those facts weren't what scared her the most.

Why couldn't she remember the accident?

More importantly, why was she missing ten months of memories? And since when did she have a fiancé?

Surely when she saw the man she was in love with, her memories would come tumbling back. Maybe, when her head quit pounding so fiercely, she'd remember everything.

She attempted to sit up as the doctor, a uniformed police officer and a tall stranger came into the room. "Julie, thank God you're all right." The very hot man clad in a pair of jeans and a black hoodie that clung to a pair of broad shoulders rushed to her side and picked up her hand.

This man, with his forest-green eyes and handsome, chiseled features was her fiancé? How had she gotten so lucky? And why, oh, why, didn't she remember anything about him?

"It's Nick, honey," he said. "You don't remember me?" Her anxiety must have shone on her face. "It's okay. Everything is going to be just fine." He released her hand and she immediately felt bereft.

"Ms. Peterson, I'm Officer Brown. Do you mind if I ask you a couple of questions?"

"No, I don't mind, but I doubt I'll be able to answer them," she said. She wished Nick would take her hand again. Even though she couldn't remember him, his hand around hers had brought her a small bit of comfort.

And she needed to be comforted at this moment. As the officer asked her questions about the accident, she tried as hard as she could to remember even the smallest detail about what had happened. But there was nothing.

"The last thing I remember is going to the Italian Gardens for my birthday. My parents were there, along with my brothers and my sister. But since my birthday is in two months from now, I'm missing almost a full year of memories."

A hollow wind blew through her as she shifted her gaze from the police officer to the doctor. "Is this kind of thing normal?" she asked, although she knew it wasn't.

"Sometimes it occurs that after a traumatic event like a car accident, the patient has no memories of that particular event," Dr. Carlson replied. "It's the way the brain protects you from emotional pain and trauma. I haven't dealt with a patient who has the kind of amnesia we're talking about here. My advice would be to go home and surround yourself with familiar things and people. Don't stress yourself and hopefully those memories will return quickly."

Hopefully? The pounding in her head intensified. She glanced back at Nick. How could she have no memories of dating, of falling in love with him? What else had happened in the ten months she'd forgotten?

"I hope your recovery happens quickly," Officer Brown said. "And now, if you'll excuse me, I have to get back to work."

"If your memories don't come back on their own within the next six to eight weeks or so, then I'll refer you to a neurologist who might be able to help," Dr. Carlson said when Officer Brown had left the room. "I recommend no driving for the next week to ten days, and you take it easy. In the meantime, you're our guest for the rest of the night."

Once again she looked at Nick. "Will you stay here with me?"

"We can get you a pillow and a blanket," Dr. Carlson said to Nick.

"Of course I'll stay," Nick replied after a moment of hesitation.

"I'll send in a nurse," Dr. Carlson replied, and then he was gone, leaving her alone with a man, a virtual stranger, who she apparently loved but didn't remember.

"I hope you don't mind staying. I feel so alone right now," she said. It was such an inadequate statement. She was overwhelmed and terrified by her brain's malfunction. How had this happened? Why had it happened? She hadn't sustained any serious injuries that might explain it.

He sat on the beige recliner next to her bed. "You aren't alone."

"Aren't you warm in that sweatshirt?" It seemed an odd choice of clothing for a July night. She only knew it was July because the doctor had told her.

"Yes, I am." He got up from the chair. "I'll be right back." He disappeared into the adjoining bathroom.

This was so awkward. He knew everything about her…about them, and she knew nothing. Her fiancé. Had a wedding date already been chosen? What did he do for a living? Did they live together? Just thinking about what she didn't know hurt her head.

Nick stepped out of the bathroom, his sweatshirt a wad in his hands. The man had been a hunk in the hoodie. He was even more so in a white T-shirt stretched tight across his shoulders and chest.

He placed the black sweatshirt on another

chair and then once again sat in the recliner. "Are you sure you can't remember anything about me?"

"Nothing. I'm so sorry, Nick. If we're engaged, then I'm sure I love you madly, but you're going to have to fill in a lot of blanks for me."

"I'll do the best I can."

"Thank God, you weren't hurt in the accident. My car...?"

"It was towed to Jerry's Ford. Tomorrow you'll need to call your insurance company to get things squared away."

"Was I still driving a blue Ford Focus?" What might have changed in the past year? Did she still live in the same house? Oh, God, had anyone she loved died?

He nodded. "That's right."

"I'm assuming I still work for my family's pawn shop, but what do you do?" It was far easier to focus on him than anything else at the moment. She couldn't think about anything else in her life right now. It was all so overwhelming.

"I'm a physical education teacher and football coach at JL Cook High School."

"That explains it," she murmured more to herself than to him. Broad shoulders, lean hips and a stomach that didn't appear to have an ounce of fat…the man appeared to have a great physique.

"Explains what?"

Heat warmed her cheeks. "Uh… You seem to be in good health." Good grief, he was probably wondering now if she not only suffered from amnesia, but also if the accident had really addled her brain.

A nurse came into the room. "Here we are," she said with a bright smile. "One pillow and a blanket." She handed the items to Nick and then turned toward Julie. "Is there anything I can get for you?"

"My memories," Julie replied with a rueful smile. "Actually, I'm fine."

"You just ring your bell if you need anything at all."

"Thank you," Julie replied. "Tell me how we met," she asked Nick when the nurse had left the room. "Was it love at first sight?"

He changed position in the chair. "We met at the little coffee shop up the street from the pawn shop." His gaze didn't quite meet hers.

"The Coffee Bean," she said.

"That's right. I saw you and asked for your number and I was shocked and happy when you gave it to me. And that was the beginning."

"Does my family like you? I mean… I know how my dad and my brothers can be." Her older brothers had never liked anyone she'd dated. Why could she remember that and yet have no memories of her fiancé?

"I haven't met any of your family and we haven't told them about us. Uh… You wanted to keep it a secret until I put a ring on your finger."

"You haven't done that?" She looked down at her hand to confirm there was no engagement ring.

"Not yet." His gaze finally met hers. "We were shopping for a ring."

"Do we live together?"

"No. You didn't want to live together before the wedding. You know, you should probably try to get some rest. It's late and, needless to say, you've been through quite a trauma." He smiled for the first time and a wave of heat swept through her. He had a gorgeous smile.

"Yes, of course." She closed her eyes but sleep was the furthest thing from her mind. She still had so many questions.

The sound of the recliner chair going to a prone position let her know he was prepared to sleep. He'd probably been terrified when she'd been unconscious in the car.

She opened her eyes and gazed over to him. He'd unfolded the blanket and put the pillow behind his head. His eyes were closed but she knew he wasn't asleep.

"Nick?"

His eyes opened and he gazed at her. Oh, she could fall into those inviting green depths.

"Yeah?"

"Tell me about the accident. What exactly happened?" She needed to know at least this much before she could fall asleep.

He released a deep sigh. "We were at your place and we had a fight."

She raised the head of her bed. "A fight about what?"

"Something stupid. Something not worth fighting about," he replied. "You like your house cool...cold to me. I got irritated that I needed to wear a sweatshirt in July just to be comfortable at your place. You got angry and got into the car. I jumped in the passenger seat and, before I knew what was happening, you hit the tree."

"Where was I going?" she asked.

"I don't know. It doesn't matter now. All that matters is that you're okay." He closed his eyes again.

She lowered the head of her bed and once

again shut her eyes. Maybe if she gave her brain a rest she'd wake up with all her memories restored.

Maybe when the sun came up in the morning she'd remember how very much she loved Nick and why. Despite the fact that she was safe and relatively unhurt, a dark fear whispered inside her.

Chapter Two

If there was prison time for lies told, throughout the long night Nick had earned a life sentence. Julie's amnesia had been both a blessing and a curse.

He now sat in the hospital cafeteria with a cup of coffee and the morning newspaper in front of him. He turned the pages slowly, a knot inside his chest as he searched for a story about a specific murder.

Had anyone seen him on the street before the accident? Had some late-night soul peeked out the window in time to see him running by? Would all of his lies come to light?

He couldn't get the vision of Brian out of his head. Who had murdered him? And what about the strange carving in his forehead? Did it mean anything or was it just a coincidence that it looked like a *V*?

He checked every single page, but there was no story in the paper about that particular murder. It was possible Brian's body hadn't even been found yet. He lived alone and Nick couldn't imagine the creep had too many friends.

But Nick couldn't be sure he was out of hot water yet. He thought of the 1970's Son of Sam killer. David Berkowitz had terrorized New York by shooting eight people before a traffic ticket had led to his arrest.

And at the moment Nick's car was parked on a residential street where it didn't belong. No, Nick wouldn't breathe easier until Brian McDowell's killer was caught. Only then would he believe he was truly safe.

He shoved the paper aside and wrapped his hands around the foam cup of coffee. The murder wasn't his only problem. Julie Peterson. He'd intentionally taken advantage of her amnesia to save his own butt, but somehow he now felt responsible for her.

She'd made it clear when she'd awakened that morning that she was depending on him to get her through this difficult period. She'd almost begged him to promise to stay close to her until her memories returned.

He'd thought to get her home from the hospital and then disappear from her life. But how could he do that to her? How could he take away the one thing she believed was true when she was obviously struggling with her missing memories?

It didn't help that she had beautiful blue eyes that held more than a touch of vulnerability. It didn't help that her heart-shaped face and spill of dark hair fired up a heat inside him he found both unexpected and unwanted. What a damn mess he'd made of things.

Right now the doctor was supposed to be writing out her release orders. They would be taking a taxi home because his car was still parked on a street where it didn't belong. He had to figure out how in the hell he was going to get it and he needed to get it as soon as possible.

Julie had complained of a headache in the wee hours of the morning and they had given her something for pain. Nick wished somebody would give him something for the festering fear that tightened his chest to the point he could scarcely breathe.

He was terrified Julie would regain her memories and yet knew the only way to exit her life was for her to regain her memories. There was nothing worse than being an attempted murderer and having a conscience. He didn't even want to think about the possibility that she already had a boyfriend. That would be a complication he definitely didn't need.

It was a damned quagmire and right now he couldn't see his way out of it. The last thing he wanted to do was to hurt Julie, who had only been an innocent victim in all this.

He hadn't slept at all through the night. If it wasn't a nurse coming in to check Julie's vitals that kept sleep at bay, it was Julie softly calling his name to make sure he was still with her.

Checking his watch, he quickly downed the last of his coffee. He needed to get back to her room. She'd be anxiously waiting for him.

And she *was* waiting for him. Perched on the edge of the bed and dressed in the jeans and sleeveless blue blouse she'd been in when she'd crashed her car, she held papers in her hand and her IV had been removed.

She stood at the sight of him, her smile filled with relief. "I'm free to go. I just have to wait for a nurse to bring in a wheelchair."

Once again he was struck by her beauty. Even with her beautiful blue eyes telegraphing a simmering panic, she was stunning. Her long, dark hair was slightly tousled. Her nose was straight and her lips were just full enough to tempt a man. If she didn't have a man in her life, he'd wonder why.

"Nick?"

She pulled him from his wayward thoughts.

"I need to use your cell phone to call for a taxi," he said.

"Of course." She dug in the purse next to her on the bed and withdrew the phone. "Want me to grab your hoodie?"

"No!" The word snapped out of him. He smiled quickly. "I'll get it. You just sit right there on the bed until your ride appears."

That was all he needed…for her to grab his sweatshirt and the gun and other items to fall out into the open.

He made the call for a taxi, his nerves once again tightening his gut.

"Here we are," a nurse named Nancy said as she pushed a wheelchair into the room. "First-class transportation for the patient."

"This really isn't necessary," Julie said.

"Hospital protocol," Nancy replied cheerfully. "No matter how you come in, you always go out in a wheelchair."

Within twenty minutes they were getting into a taxi that would take them to her house.

"I hope you can be patient with me," she said once they were under way. "I'm going to have a million questions for you." She grabbed his hand and held tight.

He tried not to remember the last time a woman had held his hand, but the memory exploded in his mind. Debbie...broken and stabbed on the marble entry floor of a vacant mansion...the odor of her blood rife in the air. Her eyes glazed as she fought to maintain consciousness. He'd fallen to her side despite the police officers attempting to keep him away.

That moment was etched deeply in his brain...the grief and the outrage, the disbelief and the overwhelming rage. He'd knelt beside her and had grasped her hand. "Debbie, who did this? Who did this to you, baby?" he'd cried.

"Winthrop." The name whispered from her just before she coughed up a mouthful of blood. Her fingers suddenly tightened around his. "Be happy," she'd said and then she was gone, forever stolen from him by an act of despicable inhumanity.

"...happy to be home." Julie's voice yanked him out of the nightmare of his past as the cab pulled to a halt in front of an attractive two-story house at the back end of a cul-de-sac.

She released his hand to get into her purse and pay the driver.

They both got out and the taxi pulled away.

Nick followed her to the front door, his chest tight with tension. Once they were inside, his lies would continue because he didn't know what else to do.

He couldn't very well confess to her the truth: that he'd used her and her accident because he'd been in the neighborhood to commit a murder and needed a fast alibi. His biggest concern now was getting his car off the residential street where it didn't belong.

She opened the front door and he followed her into an entry hall with a black-and-gray-tiled floor. She dropped her keys in a basket on a small table and then took a step into what he assumed was the living area. And gasped.

A white-brick fireplace graced one wall. A black-leather sofa sat between two glass-topped end tables. The glass coffee table held a centerpiece that showcased red and bright yellow flowers. The furnishings were modern and tasteful, but the reason for her gasp was instantly evident.

The remnants of a floor lamp lay on the

floor, the white-glass globe nothing more than glittering shards against the tiled floor. A large red candle also lay on the floor in front of the shattered glass of a painting on the wall.

She turned to look at Nick, her expression one of stunned surprise. "You said we fought..." Her voice trailed off.

He improvised. "We were both very angry. I broke the lamp and you threw the candle at the painting."

Somebody had fought in this room. Of course, he had no idea what had happened in her living room the night before. She was so vulnerable without her memories. Now he wondered if somehow Julie was in danger.

What or who had she been running from last night?

THE BROKEN LAMP and the shattered glass from the painting horrified her. She'd never been a fighter and rarely lost her temper. At least she remembered that about herself from a year ago. What had happened in the past ten months that had turned her into a woman who would throw a candle at a beautiful painting? Who apparently didn't have any control over her emotions?

Nick looked at the mess, grimaced and then gazed at her. "Let's get all this cleaned up." He set his hoodie down on one of the living room chairs.

She got a broom and dustpan from the utility room just off the kitchen and then returned to the living room where Nick had righted the floor lamp.

"This isn't who we are," he said as they worked on the cleanup. "We've both been under some stress and this was the first time something like this has ever happened between us."

His words made her feel somewhat better, but they did nothing to staunch a faint, simmering fear that had been inside her since she'd regained consciousness in the ambulance.

She knew instinctively the fear didn't come from being around Nick. Rather, strangely, he was a comfort, a solid anchor in a sea that had become alien.

They worked silently until all of the glass had been cleaned up. "I think I need to check out the whole house to orient myself," she said as she dumped the last of the glass into the trash bin.

"That sounds like a good idea," he replied. "I'll come with you."

She smiled gratefully. "I appreciate it."

Thankfully the downstairs was exactly as she remembered it to be. Her hand slid up the oak banister and with each step she wished Nick would just hold her for a moment and tell her everything was going to be all right.

She groaned faintly as she climbed upward.

"Are you okay?" he asked from behind her.

"I'm fine, just sore. I have to admit I feel like I was run over by a truck." Muscles she hadn't known she possessed now protested her movements.

"The doctor warned us that you would probably be sore for the next couple of days," he replied.

"I just hope everything up here is the same as I remember it," she said when they reached the landing. "I'd feel more centered if there aren't any more surprises."

"I hope so, too," he replied.

She breathed a quick sigh of relief as she walked straight down the hall and entered her bedroom. The coral-colored bedspread with turquoise throw pillows was achingly familiar. The knickknacks, the artwork on the wall, and the nightstands and dresser were just as she remembered them.

"You good?" he asked.

She turned and flashed him another smile. "So far, so good."

A quick glance in the other two bedrooms further assured her that at least here, in her house, nothing had changed. The room she used as her home office still had paperwork strewed across the top of the desk and the other bedroom was an attractive and clean guest room.

Even as relief winged through her, an overwhelming exhaustion struck her. Her body was sore and her brain was working too hard to remember something—anything—from the past year.

She stepped closer to Nick and wrapped her arms around his waist. She leaned into him. "Just hold me a minute, please." There was a moment of hesitation and then his arms surrounded her. Was the faint scent of his spicy cologne familiar? She wasn't sure, but it was definitely appealing.

"I'm scared, Nick," she whispered into the hollow of his throat. "I feel so lost right now. Could you stay here with me for a couple of days?"

Again, there was a small hesitation. "Of course," he replied. "But I'll need to go home and get some things." He dropped his arms to his sides and reluctantly she stepped away from him.

"I'm sorry to be a pain." She released a deep sigh. "I'm hoping my memories will return in the next day or so and then I won't be so anxious."

"It's fine. I'll just head to my house and pack up some clothes."

They walked back downstairs and it wasn't until they reached the living room again that she realized Nick didn't have his car.

"I'll need to drive you home," she said.

"No," he said sharply. He smiled then, as if aware his tone had been curt. "In case you forgot, your car is now in the shop, and besides, what you need to do is rest. It won't take me long to get to my place and get back here." He reached out and lightly touched her shoulder. "I don't want you to worry about anything. Maybe you should try to nap while I'm gone. I know you didn't get much sleep last night."

"I am exhausted," she admitted. She was definitely feeling the past night of too little sleep.

"Then get upstairs in that nice, comfortable bed and get some rest."

"You'll wake me when you get back?" she asked.

"I promise. I'll have to wake you because I don't have a key."

She looked at him in surprise. "I've never given you a key?"

"You told me you'd give me a key on the day we got married."

"Do I have a key to your house?" she asked.

"You did. I gave you one, but you lost it a couple of weeks ago. We hadn't gotten around to having another one made for you." He inched toward the front door. "Stop overthinking things and get some rest, Julie." With those words, he walked out the front door.

Immediately she felt bereft and vulnerable. For the next few minutes she wandered around the living room, touching familiar items in an effort to calm the anxiety and the crazy simmer of fear that coursed through her.

Surely these emotions were normal for somebody suffering from amnesia. Her mind wasn't her own right now. She was just grateful Nick had agreed to stay with her for the next few days. There had been comfort in his arms. That must speak to the strength of their relationship...of their love for each other.

How she wished she could remember the excitement of dating him and the joy of falling in love with him. She did remember being ready for love, wanting to get married and start a family of her own. It didn't seem fair that she remembered wanting these things but had no memory of actually finding love with the very hot physical education teacher.

She'd sensed his hesitation to touch her, to hold her, and she understood it. He was in as awkward a position as she was. He knew she didn't remember him, that he was basically a stranger to her. She was certain he didn't know exactly how to treat her.

What he didn't understand was that she took it on complete faith that he was her soul mate, otherwise she wouldn't have been working on wedding plans with him. She wouldn't be his fiancée without first knowing with utter certainty that he was the man she wanted to spend the rest of her life with. Before her accident, she'd obviously decided he was that man.

A clenched hand of anxiety continued to grip both her heart and her brain. It had been there when she'd realized she had no memories of so much time and it hadn't eased up since.

If she thought it might help to beat her fists against her skull, she'd do it. Hopefully, the doctor was right and now that she was home her memory would return quickly.

Sleep. She definitely needed to get some sleep and to stop thinking so much. Deciding to stretch out on the sofa instead of going all the way upstairs to her room, she was detoured by a flashing red light on the answering machine on one of the end tables.

Three new messages awaited her. She punched the play button.

"Hey, girly, where are you? You were supposed to open up shop this morning. Call me." It was as if she'd just heard her father's voice yesterday. Thank goodness he sounded strong and healthy.

"Where the hell are you?" The next voice spoke. "It's bad enough I usually have to cover Casey's shifts, but now you're going to be a flake, too?" The message had been left by her older brother, Max. Some things never changed and the irritation in his voice was as familiar to her as her own heartbeat.

She needed to call her family and tell them about her accident. Max should know her well enough to know she'd never shirk her responsibility at the pawn shop for no reason. She wasn't like their younger sister who often called in to get out of working. Or was she? She had no idea who she'd become over the past year.

"Don't tell."

She reeled back at the gravelly, unrecognizable voice that hissed over the machine. An icy chill instantly gripped her soul.

"You'd better not tell a soul or I promise I'll kill you."

The answering machine clicked off. Still, she remained unmoving, staring at the phone that had suddenly become an instrument of evil malevolence.

Was the call a joke? She instantly dismissed the idea. She knew instinctively that nobody she knew would think that kind of thing funny.

Oh, God, what did she know? What had she forgotten that was so important somebody would threaten to kill her to keep it a secret? Who had made that call? The Caller ID read "Anonymous."

There was no way she was going to nap, not with that horrendous voice and threat ringing in her ears. Her legs trembled beneath her as she hurried to the front door and made sure it was locked. She then returned to the family room and sank down onto the sofa.

She needed Nick. Maybe he knew what this was all about. She hoped he hurried back because she'd never been so scared in her entire life.

Chapter Three

Nick ran out of the cul-de-sac, his brain on overload. All he wanted to do at the moment was move his car off the neighborhood street where he'd parked it last night. Had it only been last night? It felt like a lifetime ago.

His nerves were totally shot. It wasn't just a lack of sleep that had him on edge. It was a combination of murder and lies that ricocheted around in his brain, leaving him with a nauseating anxiety.

First things first, he told himself. *Get the car.* He slowed his pace to a brisk walk as he reached the street where he'd parked the night before.

Relief washed over him as he saw in the distance that the car was still where he'd left it. The relief was short-lived as he drew closer and saw a man in the front yard next to where he'd parked.

His stomach knotted and his mouth dried. He'd hoped to get his car and get out of there without anyone seeing him. Hopefully, when the body was found, the police wouldn't question people this far away from the scene. Would they?

The man was an older gentleman and he held a garden hose that spewed a small stream of water on a bed of red and purple petunias. "Good morning," he said cheerfully as Nick approached the car.

"It's a fine one," Nick replied, grateful his voice held nothing of his apprehension.

"It's going to be a hot one. Stay cool and have a good day," the old man said.

"You, too," Nick replied and quickly got into the car. He set the gun with the ski mask and the gloves all wrapped in his hoodie on the passenger seat, started the engine and pulled away from the curb.

Thank God there was no parking ticket under his wiper. And thank God none of the neighbors had gotten suspicious of a strange car parked on their street and had called the cops.

He headed for home, his heart thundering as he glanced at the hoodie. He wouldn't feel better until he got rid of the gun. Even though it couldn't be traced to Brian McDowell's murder, Nick had no idea what other crime it might be traced to.

He had been instructed to throw it into the bushes at the crime scene, but when he'd seen Brian's body, rational thought had fled his brain. Also the very last thing he wanted to do now was to toss it in a place where a kid might find it.

For the first time in twelve hours he felt relatively safe as he pulled into the driveway of his brick three-bedroom ranch house. He got out of the car with the hoodie in his arms, then unlocked the door and stepped inside.

The air smelled clean…like furniture polish and bathroom cleanser. Although by no means a clean freak, he'd spent the day before cleaning the house in a frenzy to occupy his mind before heading out to murder a man.

He'd known the risks, that he might be arrested or killed himself. He'd supposed that if either of those things had happened, he'd at least be at peace that the police would find that he kept a clean house.

He sank down on his sofa and rubbed a hand across his forehead where a headache threatened. He hadn't had a chance to breathe since he'd stumbled onto Brian's dead body.

You could just stay right here, a small voice whispered. *Julie doesn't know your address. She doesn't even have your phone number.*

There was no question the thought was more than a bit appealing.

Then he thought about the hug he'd shared with her. Her slender body had felt so fragile in his arms. He'd felt not only the press of her breasts against him but also the rapid beat of her heart.

How frightening was it to wake up and lose almost a year of your life? How scary would it be to not have a single memory from that length of time? He couldn't imagine. But he'd love to go to sleep and wake up and magically lose the last three agonizing, lonely years of his life. He'd welcome the amnesia that would wipe away all memories of the brutal murder of the woman he'd loved.

Debbie. She'd been a go-getter. She'd gotten her real-estate license and had landed a job with an upscale real-estate company. She'd been dynamic and a hard worker and, within two years, she'd established herself as one of the top sellers in a four-state area. Nick had always said she could successfully sell the swamps in Florida.

Nick had loved her, but he'd grown to dislike her job, which kept her busy at all hours during the days and late evenings.

That job was what had taken her to an empty mansion to meet a potential buyer. That job was what had led to her murder. Nick shook his head to dispel his train of thoughts.

He couldn't go there. He couldn't think about her murder right now. He had bigger decisions to make at the moment. Should he just stay here or should he go back to Julie's and continue his pretense?

Debbie wouldn't want him to leave Julie hanging, especially given the fact that Nick had filled her head with a bunch of lies to save his own ass. By claiming her as his fiancée, Nick had given Julie an instant sense of false comfort.

He looked around, the very room where he sat evoking agonizing memories. He and Debbie had bought this house just before her murder. They had painted the master bedroom her favorite shade of light blue and had updated the kitchen. They had also planted a small redbud tree in the backyard. She hadn't lived long enough to see its first buds.

They had planned for children to fill the spare bedrooms. Dammit, they had planned a

life together and some man—some animal—
had taken her away from him.

He swallowed the familiar rage and got up
from the sofa. He grabbed the hoodie with the
gun, ski mask and gloves wrapped inside. He
then went into his bedroom and opened the
closet door.

On the top shelf were several folded blan-
kets. He shoved the hoodie between them,
knowing sooner or later he needed to get rid
of that damned gun.

He picked up a duffel bag and placed it
on his bed. He'd stay with Julie for a couple
of days to help her navigate. Maybe during
that time he could manipulate a fight and a
breakup. That would be the best way for him
to exit her life with no questions.

Still, when her memories returned, he'd
have some explaining to do, but he'd face
that when it happened. What concerned him
more than a little bit was the scene in her living room. What had happened there in the
minutes before she'd gotten into her car and
hit that tree? It looked like she'd fought with
somebody.

He had no idea if she was in danger or not,
but that was another reason why, in good conscience, he couldn't walk away from her yet.

It took him only minutes to pack enough clothing and toiletries for a few days away. He then left his house and got back into his car.

He turned on the radio in an effort to clear his mind from all thoughts. He didn't want to think about how screwed up everything had become.

He was exhausted. He'd gotten little sleep in the nights leading up to Brian McDowell's murder. Now he feared that any sleep he did manage to get would be haunted by the vision of the bloodbath he'd seen.

Who had committed the crime? The question thundered in his head. If it hadn't been one of the other men in their murder pact, then who else knew about their plan to get justice that had been denied?

Tightening his hands on the steering wheel, he turned into the cul-de-sac and steeled himself to tell even more lies. He parked and grabbed the duffel, then walked up to the front door and knocked.

The lock clicked, the door opened and Julie launched herself into his arms as deep sobs exploded from her.

"Hey…what's happened?" It was obvious she hadn't regained her memory, otherwise she wouldn't be in his arms right now.

She shook her head, apparently unable to speak around her tears. He dropped his duffel and hesitantly put his arms around her. "Julie, talk to me. Tell me what's going on."

What he really needed her to do was to step away from him despite the fact he'd pulled her closer into his arms. Her trembling body against his felt far too warm as he became aware of the faint, attractive floral scent that emanated from her.

As if she read his mind, she took a step backward and instead grabbed his hand and held tight as he picked up his bag once again. She then led him into the living room. She dropped his hand and pointed to the telephone answering machine on the end table.

"What is it?" he asked. A new tension tightened his stomach. What now? As if this whole situation wasn't complicated enough.

Julie stared at him with wide, tear-filled eyes. "The last message. You need to listen to it." She made no move to approach the phone, but instead stared at it as unmistakable fear leaped into her eyes.

With a sense of dread, Nick walked over to the machine and punched the appropriate button so he could hear the message. As the rasping voice filled the room, Julie sank down on the sofa and began to quietly cry again.

Fear replaced his sense of dread. The venom-filled voice hadn't issued just a warning…it sounded like a promise. What in the hell was going on? He'd escaped one murder scene only to walk into another potentially deadly mystery.

"You don't recognize the voice?" he asked. He hadn't even been able to tell if it was a man or a woman. It had obviously been computer distorted.

Once again she shook her head and wiped the tears from her cheeks with her fingertips. "I don't know the voice and I don't remember what I'm not supposed to tell. I was hoping you could tell me. Did I share with you anything that might explain the call?"

He sank down next to her, wondering what in the hell he'd gotten himself into. "No, I don't have a clue. You never mentioned anything to me about any kind of a dangerous secret."

"I'm in a nightmare," she said softly. "I'm in a damned nightmare and I can't wake up. I can't tell what I don't remember and how will the caller know I have amnesia?"

"We should call the police." As much as Nick didn't want any authorities involved with him, this sounded serious and he couldn't—he wouldn't—choose his own safety over hers. She didn't deserve that.

"No, I don't want to talk to the police," she surprised him by saying. She rubbed two fingers in the center of her forehead. "I'm not sure why, but my gut is telling me I don't want the police involved in this. Besides, what could they do? It was an anonymous call. It would be easy to write it off as some kind of a terrible prank. They aren't going to put manpower and effort into figuring it out and, without my memories, I can't help them at all."

She reached for his hand and her fingers clung around his tightly. Her blue eyes gazed at him with love...and need. "I'm just so grateful I have you, Nick. I don't know what I'd do right now without you."

He squeezed her hand. "I'm here and nobody is going to hurt you as long as I'm around."

An overwhelming sense of resignation swept through him. Damned. He had a feeling he was damned if he stayed with her and damned if he left.

JULIE BOLTED UP with a scream on her lips. Instead of releasing it, she gasped, her racing heart making it difficult for her to draw in a full breath. Her bedsheets were twisted around her thighs, as if attempting to keep her in the nightmare she now couldn't remember.

Morning light drifted through her thin, lacy bedroom curtains as her heartbeat slowly returned to normal. She drew in several deep breaths.

What had she dreamed? It had obviously been a nightmare. Otherwise she wouldn't have awakened with the taste of fear lingering in her mouth and a scream begging to be released.

Disappointment washed over her as no memories of the past ten months had come to her with sleep. But what she remembered vividly was the frightening phone call promising her death if she told what she knew.

What did she know? What secret was trapped in the darkness of her mind that was worth her death? Was she safe because she couldn't tell anyone? Would the caller leave her alone if she didn't spill whatever secret the caller thought she knew? Was that what she had dreamed about?

Nick. Just thinking his name caused a

calming effect even though the night before had been a bit awkward. She'd just assumed he would stay in her room and sleep in her bed with her. Despite having no memories of him, she was fine with that. But he'd insisted he stay in her guest room.

She knew he was only thinking about her and she appreciated that, but it would have been nice to go to sleep last night with his big, strong arms around her. Maybe then she wouldn't have suffered from a nightmare.

She glanced over at the clock on the nightstand. It was a few minutes after seven. She'd called her father last night to tell him about her accident and her stolen memories. He'd immediately declared a family meeting at her place at eight thirty this morning.

It would be the first time her family met her fiancé. She hoped they weren't too hard on him, but the Peterson family was definitely loud and opinionated. And, as far as she could remember, they had never liked anyone she had dated, not that she had dated that often.

She got out of bed and went into the adjoining bathroom. Twenty minutes later she was showered and dressed. The scent of coffee met her as she headed down the stairs, letting her know Nick was already up.

She walked into the kitchen to find him seated at the table, a cup of fresh brew in front of him. "Good morning," he said with a smile.

"Good morning to you," she replied and beelined to the cabinet where the coffee cups were stored. He was a welcome sight, his buff body clad in a pair of jeans and a navy T-shirt that stretched across his broad shoulders.

Her heart fluttered a bit in her chest. There was no question that she was intensely physically drawn to him even without her memories. But what woman wouldn't be attracted to such a good-looking man?

"How are you feeling?" Nick asked as she joined him at the table.

"Pretty well, except for the memory thing. How did you sleep?"

"I slept fine." He took a sip of his coffee.

"Are you ready for the onslaught of my family?"

"I have to admit I'm a little nervous," he replied.

"Oh, Nick, it will be fine. I can't imagine a single reason why they won't like you. Besides, it's time to meet them. We've been dating a long time and talking about marriage."

He nodded and his gaze went to his coffee.

She took a sip of hers and continued to look at him over the rim of her cup. She still had a hard time believing this terrific guy was in love with her, but it must be so. Otherwise he wouldn't be here with her now.

"We have time for a quick breakfast before my family arrives. I'm sorry, I don't know what you like to eat."

He looked up and smiled once again. "I'm not much of a breakfast eater. I'm generally good with just a couple cups of coffee."

"Me, too." She was ridiculously pleased that they had even this relatively small thing in common. "There are so many things I don't know about you. Do you have a big family?"

His eyes darkened slightly. "No. It's just me. My parents were killed four years ago in a car accident and I didn't have any siblings."

"Oh, Nick, I'm so sorry."

The smile he offered her wasn't as big as the last one. "Thanks, but it was a long time ago."

It might have been a long time ago, but it looked like raw grief that had momentarily darkened his eyes.

"This is all so awkward," she said in an effort to change the subject. "You probably know everything there is to know about me and I don't know anything about you except for the really important things."

One of his dark brows quirked upward. "Important things?"

She nodded. "You must be a good man. You are kind and good and love me passionately. I wouldn't have dated you so long and agreed to marry you if you weren't that kind of person."

He frowned and shifted positions in the chair. "I'm no saint, Julie. And while you can't remember me, don't try to make me into one."

She raised her chin and smiled at him. "Okay, but I stand by my feelings. I know who you are at your core, Nick. I wouldn't have settled for less."

He drained his coffee cup and jumped up. "Is there anything we need to do to prepare for your family?"

"Make a fresh pot of coffee," she replied. "Unless something drastic changed in the past year, my family chugs coffee like it's the fountain of youth."

"You sit tight, I'll make a fresh pot," he replied. "And while I'm doing that you can give me a quick refresher on your family members."

She took another sip from her cup, set it down and then leaned back in the chair. "I can only tell you what I remember about them from a year ago."

Grief and anger suddenly rose up in the back of her throat. Grief over the missing memories of the people she loved, and anger that her brain continued to betray her by not functioning right.

Nick poured the water into the coffee machine and then turned back to face her expectantly.

"George is my father and he runs the business and us with a heavy hand. Lynetta is my mother. She's loud and opinionated and as tough as Dad. Max is my oldest brother and he's just like my father...they both have a lot of bark, but not too much bite. Then there's Tony who is a year older than me. He's quiet and, like me, doesn't like confrontation. Finally, there's Casey. She's the baby of the family and is the apple of my parents' eyes."

She couldn't help the smile that curved her

lips as she thought of her baby sister. "She's also spoiled and wild, a bit lazy and totally gorgeous."

"And all of you work at the pawn shop," Nick said.

She nodded. "That pawn shop isn't just our business, it's a family legacy of sorts. My grandfather started it, but it was Dad who built it into the largest pawn shop in Kansas City."

"Everyone has heard of Peterson Pawn, but I've never been inside the store."

"Once you meet my family I'll take you in with me and give you the grand tour." Once again a roll of emotions swept through her. What had changed at the store over the past ten months? What had happened in her family's life that she couldn't remember?

Had Max finally found somebody to date? What about her other siblings? Max and Tony hadn't even been dating anyone ten months before. Casey was the only one in the family who dated often, exchanging men as quickly as she changed her nail color. Had Julie gone to a wedding? Had she been Casey's maid of honor like the two of them had always promised each other?

She wanted to pull her brain out of her

skull and shake it violently until it started working right again. What was the amnesia protecting her from? A car accident?

Don't tell. The two words thundered in her head, momentarily stealing her breath as an icy hand gripped her heart.

"Julie? Are you all right?" Nick gazed at her with a touch of concern.

"I'm fine." She forced a smile as she stood. "I'm just going to set out some cups and cream and sugar for when the family arrives."

"Can I help?"

"No, thanks. I've got it." She needed to do something to keep the simmering fear in her at bay. Not only was she afraid of the phone threat, now a new rivulet of anxiety swept through her as she prepared for her family to arrive.

She placed the cups on the countertop and then turned to face him once again. "How do you feel about little white lies?"

"What are you talking about?" He said the words slowly…a bit warily.

"I was just thinking that I'd like to tell my family we've been dating for well over a year. I don't want them to know I have no memories of you. That will just complicate things with them."

He leaned back in the chair and nodded. "If that makes you feel better, then I don't see why we can't tell that little white lie."

She sighed in relief. She loved her family, and her father and mother had raised them to be loyal to each other and to the pawn shop. She'd never made trouble. She'd worked long hours and done everything she could to be an obedient daughter.

She might not know what had gone on for the past ten months in her life, but one thing she knew for certain...if they made her choose between them and Nick, she wanted her man.

Chapter Four

"Who in the hell are you?" George Peterson was a tall man with broad shoulders and a slight paunch. As he glared at Nick, he raised his square chin as if in anticipation of a brawl.

He and his wife, Lynetta, had entered the house without so much as a knock and now stood just inside the kitchen.

"Dad, be nice," Julie said with what sounded like a nervous laugh. "Sit down and I'll get you both some coffee while we wait for everyone else."

George didn't move. Nick walked over to him and extended his hand. "I'm Nick Simon. It's nice to meet you."

George hesitated a moment and then shook hands. Nick couldn't help but notice the rolled-up morning paper in George's hand. When Nick had awakened earlier than Julie, the first thing he'd wanted to do was to check the morning news, but he hadn't been able to find the remote for the television.

"Sit down, George," Lynetta said as she took a seat at the table.

He moved to a chair next to his wife and placed the paper in the center. "I brought in your morning paper."

"To heck with the paper," Lynetta said. Her dark eyes lingered on Julie. "What I want to know is why you didn't call us immediately from the hospital last night after your wreck."

"Everything happened so fast," Julie replied as she poured coffee for her mother and father.

Once again Nick was struck by Julie's prettiness. Clad in a pink T-shirt and a pair of jeans that hugged her slender hips and long legs, there was no question that physically she stirred something in him. Her dark hair hung down just beneath her shoulders, looking shiny and soft.

It surprised him. She couldn't have been more different than the woman who had been his wife. Debbie had been blond and was always fighting with her weight, not that Nick had cared. Debbie had been short while Julie was tall and willowy.

Julie had just finished pouring coffee for

her parents when Max and Tony came in. The two looked remarkably alike. They both had dark hair and eyes, but while Tony greeted him amicably, Max had a wealth of suspicion in his eyes.

Nick had just taken a seat at the table when Casey arrived. The long-haired, curvy young woman swept in and, with a dramatic wail, embraced Julie. "Daddy told us you hit a tree. You could have been killed." She released her sister. "What were you thinking?"

"I don't know," Julie confessed. "In fact, I don't have any memories of the past ten months."

"Before we get to that, let's talk about the white elephant in the room." Max looked pointedly at Nick. "This is supposed to be a family meeting."

"And soon he's going to be family. Everyone, this is Nick and he's my fiancé," Julie said.

Chaos broke out. Everyone talked at once until Lynetta raised her hands. "Everybody shut up," she yelled. Surprisingly everyone did. She looked at Julie. "And how is it that you have a fiancé we didn't know about?"

"Yeah, I can't believe you didn't even tell

me," Casey added. "I thought we shared all of our secrets."

"I totally get why she kept it a secret," Tony said. "Every man Julie has ever dated, you all have chased off."

"Nick isn't going anywhere," Julie replied with a warm smile at him.

A sick guilt surged up inside him. Now there were more people to lie to and Julie gazed at him with such certainty, such open trust.

He was trying to be present for Julie, but it was becoming way more difficult than he'd anticipated. Besides, more than anything, he wanted to grab the newspaper from the center of the table and see if Brian McDowell's murder had made the news.

Her family members began to fire questions at him. Where did he work? How long had he held that job? Where did he live? What did he love about Julie? He answered them all as truthfully as he could.

"I'd like to know about your financial situation," George said. "One day Julie will own part of the business. That makes her quite a catch for somebody who has nothing."

"Dad! Enough," Julie finally said in protest.

"I want to know more about this memory

loss thing," Max said. "Is it really true that you don't remember the last ten months?"

"It's true, but we're hoping that I'll get my memories back very soon," she replied.

"That's so weird," Casey said and gazed at her sister as if she were an alien from another planet.

"Weird or not, what I need to know is if you're okay to take your shift tomorrow," George said. "You're on the schedule to open and work until five."

"Please don't tell me I have to start covering your shifts. It's bad enough I have to cover for the baby half the time." Max shot a pointed glare at Casey.

Was Nick the only one who saw the dark hesitation that leaped into Julie's eyes as one of her hands rose to the base of her throat?

"What do you say, girly?" George persisted.

Julie's hand dropped to her side and she raised her chin. "As long as nothing has changed in the last year at the store, then I'll definitely be at work tomorrow."

Nick couldn't believe her family didn't think it a good idea for her to take a little time off given she'd been in a serious accident and had missing memories. But he kept his mouth shut. He didn't know enough about Julie or her family to form an opinion, although he wasn't especially eager to be friends with a man who called his daughter "girly."

George shoved back from the table and everyone else rose as a unit. Lynetta gave Julie a quick hug and George cast Nick a dark stare. "The verdict is still out on you," he said.

Nick merely nodded in return and then they were all gone. "Why didn't you tell them you weren't really ready to return to work yet?" he asked.

"Was it that obvious?" she asked as she led him into the living room.

"Apparently only to me." He eased down opposite her on the sofa.

"It will be fine and it's not as if I have any real physical injuries. I've been working in the pawn shop since I was fourteen. I could do the work there in my sleep."

"You still should have told them you needed a few more days of recovery," Nick replied. "Remember the doctor said you needed time to rest."

She shrugged. "It will be okay." A worry line darted across her forehead. "I just realized again that I don't have my car."

"Don't worry, I'll take you and pick you up from work. That's probably for the best right now anyway." He didn't want to remind her of the strange and threatening phone call from the night before, but it was obvious that's exactly what he had done.

Her bright eyes changed to a midnight blue and she wrapped her arms around herself as if she'd just experienced a deep chill. "I can't lie. I don't mind you having my back right now until I remember what I'm not supposed to talk about."

"I've got your back." Meeting her family had been a particular kind of torment for him. It had been one thing to lie to Julie but quite another to lie to her entire family.

She rose suddenly. "I know it hasn't been that long since I got out of bed but, if you don't mind, I think I'll go upstairs and lie down for a little while. I have a bit of a headache starting."

He jumped up. "Is there anything I can do for you? Do you need anything?"

"No, but thank you for asking." She gave him a warm look that once again stirred a touch of desire that he didn't want and tried to ignore.

He watched as she went slowly up the stairs. When she disappeared from view he raced back into the kitchen. He grabbed the rolled-up newspaper and sat.

His heart pounded as he unfurled the paper and checked the front page. The usual head-lines...sports, politics and advertising. Ten-sion pressed tight in his chest as he turned to the second page. And there it was, at the bot-tom of the page: Northland Man Murdered.

Nick read the article that reported Brian McDowell's death. His body had been found by a friend. The news said that he had been killed by having his throat slashed, but men-tioned nothing about the strange carving in Brian's forehead. Apparently law-enforce-ment officials were keeping that fact close to their chests.

Nick's heart nearly stopped as he contin-ued to read. A witness had come forward to report that he'd seen a man dressed in black running away from McDowell's house. Po-lice were asking anyone with information to come forward.

Had the witness seen him? Or had he seen the real killer escaping from the scene? If it had been Nick who'd been seen, had it been before or after he'd torn off his ski mask? When had he taken off the ski mask? He couldn't remember right now with the dread that coursed through his veins.

As much as he hated it, this act as Julie's fiancé was the only thing that might save him from a murder charge. He slowly closed the paper. Right now it was in his best interest for Julie not to retrieve her missing memories. But, no matter how it worked out, there was still another victim in this mess.

If Julie regained her memories, it was possible she would turn him into the police, and her heart would probably be broken by the realization that there was no love, no engagement and no talks of marriage.

He was sorry as hell that he'd drawn her into all of this. In doing so he'd not only doomed himself, but her, as well.

"SINCE I SLEPT through lunch and you had to help yourself, I was thinking maybe I'd cook a couple of steaks on the grill and we could eat out on the deck this evening," Julie said hours later when she was awake from her nap. She had gone upstairs and contacted her insurance agent to get things moving on repairing her car, then had slept half the day away.

"Sounds good to me. Just tell me what I can do to help." Nick rose from the sofa.

"You can sit back down and relax. I've got this," Julie replied.

"Are you sure you feel up to it?"

She smiled at him. "It's amazing what a long nap can do. Besides, I want to make a good meal for my man." And she hoped at the end of the evening her fiancé would at least kiss her. She yearned for some kind of physical interaction with him.

"Could you turn on the television for me? I wasn't able to find the remote," he said.

"Oh, of course." She should have thought about it earlier. He'd been sitting on the sofa with nothing to do for most of the day while she'd taken her nap. "I'm so sorry you couldn't even turn it on while I slept."

She walked over to the coffee table where there was a hidden drawer in the center. She took out the remote, turned on the television and then handed it to him. She stood close enough to him she could smell the spicy scent of his cologne. "Feel free to put on whatever you want. I'll be in the kitchen if you need anything."

Within minutes she was working to prepare an early evening meal. As she worked, she thought of the dreams she'd had while she'd napped.

They had been flaming-hot visions of her and Nick making love. They had been erotic dreams and she didn't know if they were simple longing or memories.

All she knew for sure was that they had made her want Nick. She knew he was keeping his distance as a sign of respect for her and her missing memories, but that didn't stop her from wanting him.

Maybe tonight, she told herself as she scrubbed two big baking potatoes. She'd make him a good meal and then at bedtime she'd tell him she wanted him in her bed. She'd convince him that her missing memories weren't important. Whatever her brain had forgotten, she believed her heart remembered.

Thank goodness the cat was out of the bag where Nick and her parents were concerned. He'd handled them as well as anyone could. Although she had a feeling if her father caught her alone she'd be in for an in-depth interrogation about Nick.

She'd always had a feeling her parents would be just fine if she never married. That way she could devote all her time and attention to the pawn shop forever.

Maybe it was good for right now that she

couldn't remember anything. How could her father interrogate her if she had no memories?

Within a half an hour the salad was made and in the fridge, the potatoes were baking in the oven, and the steaks had been marinated and awaited the grill.

She returned to the living room and sat next to Nick on the sofa. "I figure we'll eat in about an hour and I thought it might be nice to sit outside on the deck."

"Sounds good to me."

"What are you watching?"

He lowered the television volume. "Nothing really. I was just kind of surfing the channels for some local news, but all I'm finding is talk shows and game shows."

"Are you a news fanatic?" There were so many things she didn't remember about him.

"I wouldn't call myself a fanatic, but I like to know what's going on in the community. I want to make sure my kids at the high school don't get into any stupid trouble."

"Oh, Nick, I haven't even thought about the fact that you're a coach. Haven't football practices already begun?" She hadn't realized about how her neediness might be screwing with his life and work. Normally she wasn't so selfish.

"Actually, the practices start the last week of July, so I've still got two weeks of relatively free time left," he said.

"And hopefully before the practices begin I'll have all my memories back." She held his gaze for a long moment. "I can't wait to remember every single thing about you…about us."

"It will all eventually come to you. I peeked outside the window earlier to take a look at your deck. Do you need me to light the barbecue grill?"

"I can do it." She offered him another smile. He seemed so sober, so…distant at the moment. "I'm one of those women who doesn't mind playing with fire if a grilled steak is the end reward."

"Then, if you don't mind, I'm going to run upstairs and take a quick shower." He got up from the couch.

"Of course I don't mind. Despite everything that's happened, I'm sure you always considered this like a second home and I want you to continue to do so."

A touch of warmth lit his eyes. "I won't be long."

She nodded, her heart fluttering unexpectedly as she watched him walk up the stairs.

Her racing heart was simply affirmation that she loved Nick and that she wanted him. And he must want her, too. He was here with her right now and he didn't appear to be going anywhere anytime soon.

She got up and started back to the kitchen. She'd only made it halfway there when a vision exploded in her brain. She was alone in the pawn shop with only the security lights on. Her knees weakened. *Danger!* The word exploded in her head as fear clenched her stomach into a hard knot. Her mouth dried and a cold sweat washed over her.

Reaching for the back of the chair to steady herself, the vision vanished as quickly as it had appeared, but left behind a terror that tightened up the back of her throat.

Just a strange vision? Or had it been a flash of memory? *Don't tell.* The words thundered in her head as she finally reached the kitchen and leaned with her back against the countertop.

Had something happened at the pawn shop with one of the customers? Certainly over the years she'd dealt with all kinds of people there. She drew several long, deep breaths until the last of the feeling faded away.

She grabbed a soapy sponge from the sink

and carried it to the door that led out onto her deck, still trying to make sense of the vision her mind had momentarily presented to her.

At least this was a hopeful sign that more memories would come. Still, she had a feeling if she tried too hard to remember, then nothing would happen.

She began to clean off the round patio table with its bright red umbrella. The chairs held pads that were red and turquoise. The recliner nearby had the same patterned pad on it.

One thing she definitely remembered was how much she loved her deck. It was a large space with steps that led to her heavily treed backyard. She was lucky that the property behind hers was a green space where nothing would ever be built and the forest-like area would remain.

More than once early in the mornings or at twilight she'd seen a herd of deer appear. Right now birds sang from the trees and her anxiety of moments earlier slowly ebbed away.

This had always been a place of peace for her after a stressful day at work, although she often didn't get a chance to enjoy it. She did remember how long hours at the shop ate into any free time.

She'd just cleaned off and set the table when Nick stepped out the back door. "Thank goodness it's cooled off a little bit," he said.

Oh, my, she didn't feel cooled off at all as she looked at him. His dark hair was damp and slightly tousled. The faint five-o'clock shadow he'd worn before his shower was now gone. He'd changed from his jeans into a pair of black shorts that displayed athletic, tanned legs. His short-sleeved, white-and-black shirt showed off his muscled biceps.

"Julie?" He raised a brow quizzically.

She realized she'd been staring at him. She only hoped her mouth hadn't been hanging open. "Sorry." Her cheeks flushed warmly. "Yes, it's nice it isn't as hot as it's been. There's a nice breeze blowing."

"It's beautiful out here." He walked over to the railing and looked out to the backyard. "I envy you all these woods. This is the best kind of scenery."

She picked up the long flame ignitor she'd carried out earlier. "I agree. You don't have trees in your yard?"

"Just one, a pretty little redbud tree." His jaw tightened and he grabbed the lighter out of her hand. "I'll light the grill for you."

He stalked over to the barbecue grill. As

he lit the gas burner, his motions were stiff and unnatural.

"Nick, is something wrong?" she asked.

He jerked around to face her and, for just a brief moment, his expression was one of deep torment. The tense muscles in his face immediately relaxed into a smile. "Nothing is wrong," he replied. "Do you want to cook the steaks or do you want me to?"

"I'll do it. I noticed there was beer in the refrigerator. Why don't I bring you one and you can talk to me while the steaks grill?"

"I'll grab the beers," he replied.

She followed him into the house, wondering if she was losing her mind. Had she only imagined that look of anguish? Was her rattled brain tricking her? Unfortunately, she didn't have the answer.

Any concern she had slipped away as they sat at the table to enjoy the meal. The beer was cold and the steaks were grilled perfectly. The baked potatoes were also cooked to perfection and the conversation was light and easy.

"I think I had a memory a little while ago," she said.

"What did you remember?" He leaned forward in his chair, his gaze intent on her. He had the most intense green eyes.

She picked up her beer bottle and downed the last swallow. "It was just a flash. I was walking into the kitchen and suddenly I was in the pawn shop." A chill danced up her spine. "And I was terrified."

He studied her features. "Did you have any idea of why you were so afraid?"

"No, it came and went too quickly. There weren't enough details." She released a sigh of frustration. "I wish I would have remembered, then maybe I would know what I'm not supposed to tell."

"What could be such a big secret at the pawn shop?"

She released a wry laugh. "Right now, your guess is as good as mine."

"I've never been in a pawn shop. What kind of people come in to do business with you?"

Evening was falling and the breeze had stopped blowing. The result was an oppressive heat and humidity. "Why don't we move inside and have a cup of coffee?" she suggested. "It's starting to feel a little close out here."

"Works for me," he replied.

For the next fifteen minutes they worked

together to clear the dishes and clean the kitchen. Their previous conversation didn't resume again until they were both seated on the sofa with coffee cups in hand.

"You asked me about the people who come into the pawn shop. Some are really nice and I know they're just desperate for some quick cash to tide them over until their next payday or social security check comes in. These are the people we always hope pay their pawn on time so they won't lose their items."

She paused a moment to take a sip of her coffee and then continued. "Other customers are just a little bit weird, bringing in bizarre items to pawn or sell. But some of the clientele are definitely a bit scary."

"Scary how?"

"I think we have a lot of drug addicts desperate for their next fix. They argue about how much their item is worth, some of them get really angry that we won't front them more money." She frowned, remembering how many times she'd been a bit half scared while working.

"Do you have security in the store?"

"The only security is a bulletproof glass and a good lock on the office area. But nobody really ever works alone. Dad always makes sure when Casey or I work, one of the men works with us." She looked at him curiously. "Didn't we ever talk about my work before?"

He shifted positions and reached for his cup from the coffee table. "Rarely. You always told me you wanted to leave your work at the store and just enjoy the time we spent together."

She nodded, knowing that about herself. "What about you? Tell me about your students and your ballplayers."

For the next two hours they talked. He entertained her with stories of working with high school students and it was obvious he loved what he did. In turn she told him about some of the more colorful characters who came into the shop.

Their shared laughter made her want him even more. He was the man she'd intended to marry, a man she'd dated for a considerable amount of time.

When had they last made love? The night before her car wreck? The week before? Didn't he want her? He hadn't even kissed her since the accident. Maybe she was like Sleeping Beauty and all she needed was a kiss from her prince to bring back all her memories.

Nick stifled a yawn with the back of his hand. "Sorry," he said with a sheepish grin.

"It's getting late and I've got a morning shift at the store tomorrow."

"I still think you should have told your family you needed a few more days of rest," he replied.

"I don't like to make waves." She leaned forward and placed her hand on his arm. "Nick, why don't you sleep with me tonight?"

His muscles tightened beneath her touch. "Julie, I'm just not comfortable with that kind of intimacy when you can't even remember anything about me." He rose from the sofa. "We'll have time for that when your memories return."

She also stood. She wanted to argue with him. She wanted him to know that it was okay with her. But he'd spoken his words with a finality that brooked no discussion.

"I just feel so...so disconnected from everything and everyone." She held his gaze for an intense moment, longing for his arms around her. "Could you just...just kiss me?" An embarrassed laugh escaped her. "God, I sound so pathetic right now."

His features softened as he reached out for her and pulled her into an embrace.

She pressed into him, loving the feel of his hard, muscled chest against hers and the way his now familiar scent enveloped her.

"It's all going to be just fine," he murmured, his breath a warm caress against her forehead. "You're going to get your memories back and that will solve the mystery of the secret you know."

She raised her face and he lowered his lips to hers. It was obvious he meant it to be a quick, chaste kiss, but she would never be happy with that.

She raised her arms to his neck and opened her mouth, encouraging him to deepen the kiss. With a faint groan, he complied. His tongue swirled lazily with hers, igniting a flame in the very depths of her.

She wanted the kiss to last forever, but all too quickly he pulled away from her. Still, she was rewarded by a sweet desire that flowed from his eyes for just a moment. He did want her.

"Good night, Julie. I'll check the doors to make sure they're all locked. You can go ahead and get ready for bed."

She nodded, for a moment speechless by the flood of longing inside her. She headed for the stairs thinking she now had a new reason to want her memories back as soon as possible. When that happened, she knew Nick would take her to bed.

Chapter Five

Nick climbed the stairs fifteen minutes after Julie. How could she be so trusting as to want him in her bed when she couldn't remember anything about him?

And now that he'd kissed her, he wasn't sure how long he could stay strong against her obvious desire for him. It had been years since he'd had sex and there was no question that he was intensely drawn to Julie.

He'd love to have her in bed, with her dark hair splayed across the pillow and her body sleek and naked beneath his. It would just be a sexual release for him and nothing more. His love for his wife would always fill his heart to the point that there wouldn't be room for anyone else. His grief and rage over losing Debbie would always keep his heart firmly closed.

The problem was that his lies to Julie had

been too good. She'd believed him hook, line and sinker. It was only natural that she'd want to kiss her fiancé. It was only natural she would want to make love to the man she intended to marry and spend the rest of her life with. How long could he put her off and not give in to his own crazy desire for her?

Thankfully, he didn't have to pass Julie's bedroom to get to his own. He used the bathroom across the hall from his room to brush his teeth and then returned to the room he'd been using while here.

It was a nice bedroom, decorated in shades of cool greens and white...the colors to soothe and calm. But as he climbed into bed, he had a feeling nothing could calm him tonight.

All day long his emotions had been all over the place. He'd awakened both anxious that she'd regained her memories with sleep and nervously wondering if Brian's murder would be reported. The anxiety had shifted to fear when he'd realized not only had it been in the newspaper but there had also been a witness who had seen somebody running away.

He'd held that emotion in check and had actually managed to relax while Julie was napping. The minute she'd walked down the stairs, a new tension had struck him...the nervous energy of a man pretending to be what he wasn't.

When he'd mentioned the redbud tree in his yard, he hadn't expected the rich, raw rage and the anguish of loss that had momentarily swept through him.

Now, as he tried to get to sleep, the final emotion of the day was desire. Kissing Julie had been a huge mistake. Her lips had been soft and warm and oh, so inviting. It would have been so easy to just let himself go to her room and have sex with her.

It wasn't just that mysterious sexual draw that enticed him. She had a wonderful sense of humor. She also had a softness of spirit, just a hint of vulnerability he suspected had been with her before the accident and the troubling phone call.

The phone call. Was it possible it had been nothing more than a wrong number? Some sort of a sick prank? The caller hadn't mentioned Julie by name. Still, he couldn't dismiss the signs of some sort of altercation in her living room. What was that about? So many questions with no answers.

And how soon might a police officer knock on this door after finding him not at his house after somehow connecting him to Brian's murder? Was it even possible something like that could happen?

Had he dropped DNA while he'd stood there panting and staring at Brian's body? Would Officer Brown have questions for the man who'd been wearing a hoodie in the middle of July just down the street from a murder scene?

With too many questions whirling around in his head, he finally fell into a troubled sleep. The nightmares began almost instantly.

HE WALKED ALONG a deserted highway and just ahead a neon sign flashed with the words Don't Tell. *The building looked like a motel and he desperately needed a motel. He'd been walking this highway at night for years and he just wanted to rest.*

When he reached the structure it was, indeed, the Don't Tell Motel. With a sigh of relief he entered the lobby. It was dark and dank, a layer of smoke swirling in the air. A man stood, his back to Nick, at the registration desk. "Got your room all ready for you, Coach," he said. "Room seven."

He turned around and it was Brian McDowell, his throat torn open and bleeding, the V in his forehead oozing blood. Nick reeled backward in horror and ran outside.

He raced to room seven and threw open the door. Debbie was on the floor next to the bed, broken and bloody. "No," he screamed in rage. Before he could reach Debbie, her features transformed into Julie's.

HE SNAPPED AWAKE, his body bathed in sweat and his heart thundering madly. He panted as if he'd been running for miles and it took a moment for him to orient himself.

He jumped out of the bed. Just a dream. No, a nightmare. He wiped his hand through his sweaty hair as his body began to cool off. He glanced at the clock on the nightstand: 5:30 a.m.

Normally he would be up around six. There was no point in trying to sleep again. Besides, if he did, he feared the nightmares might find him again.

He grabbed clean clothes from the closet and then silently crept into the bathroom across the hall. Hopefully, a quick shower wouldn't waken Julie.

Instead he took an unusually long shower, hoping to rinse the last of the nightmare from his mind. It had left him feeling unsettled and on edge.

Once he was dressed, he crept quietly down the stairs and into the kitchen where he got the coffee started.

Waiting for it to brew, he moved over to the window and stared outside. Dawn's light was just barely peeking over the horizon.

Julie's shift at the pawn shop started at nine and she wouldn't get off work until five. He knew what he needed to do during the long hours of the day.

He needed to touch base with Jason Cook and Matt Tanner, the other football coaches who worked with him at the high school. With practices starting in ten days, he needed to let them know he might not be participating in the sessions, at least initially, due to a personal crisis. Julie's continued amnesia had become his crisis the minute he'd told her the first lie.

Still, even if he didn't attend the practices, he could swing by his house and grab the DVDs of last year's games. He could then work on new plays that hopefully would keep the team winning games through the coming year.

He turned away from the window, poured

a cup of coffee, then carried it to the table where he sat. It was ludicrous that he was thinking about football games when there were so many other, much bigger, issues going on right now.

Hell, for all he knew there might be a knock on the door at any time. A police officer could take him in for a lineup where a witness could positively identify him as the man seen running from Brian McDowell's on the night of the murder.

Or Julie's memories could suddenly return and she could call the police on him because he'd lied to her and she'd realized she didn't know him at all.

He both wanted and dreaded her regaining her memories. He wanted it for her, so she wouldn't feel so vulnerable and afraid living in her own skin. He dreaded it for him, not knowing what might happen when the truth finally came out.

Of course, he'd never tell anyone that he was at McDowell's house that night. Nobody would ever know he'd carried a gun, pulled on a ski mask and adorned gloves with the intention of murdering the man. That was a secret he would take to his very grave.

Another question whirling around in his

mind…since somebody else had murdered Brian, did that mean nobody would kill the man who had raped and murdered his wife?

Nick tightened his hands around his coffee cup as the familiar raw rage swept through him. The survivors group he'd attended had talked about all the stages of grief.

He'd sat at those meetings every other week for months and had been unable to understand how anyone who had lost somebody to a violent crime ever moved past the stage of anger. He embraced the anger. He couldn't move into acceptance until he got his vengeance.

"Good morning." Julie walked into the kitchen clad in a short, lightweight, pink robe. Her hair was slightly tousled from sleep and a warm smile played on her lips.

Where Nick's stomach had clenched with his rage, it now tightened for an entirely different reason. Her scent eddied in the air, that light floral smell he found so wildly attractive.

"You're up early," he said, grateful his voice didn't betray any of the anger that had gripped him a moment before or of the swift desire her presence had stirred.

"So are you," she replied. She walked over to the coffeemaker and reached up in the cabinet to retrieve a cup. The action gave him a tantalizing view of her long, bare legs.

"Did you sleep well?" She poured her coffee and then sat in the chair opposite him.

"It was a toss-and-turn kind of night," he admitted.

Her smile faded. "I'm taking up too much of your time and energy. I'm sure you have other things to do besides babysitting me. I'll be fine here alone, if you want to go back to your house."

She wouldn't be fine. The slight tremble in her voice let him know the last thing she wanted right now was to be there all alone. "I'm right where I need to be," he replied. "However, if you don't mind, I'm going to bring over some football DVDs to study when you're at work."

"Of course I don't mind. Besides, I love football. Did I ever go to any of the high school games?"

He shook his head. "You were always scheduled to work at the shop on game nights."

She sighed. "And even if I had asked for the night off, Dad would have told me no and given me a big lecture about how the business was more important than anything else in life." She took a sip of her coffee and then continued. "I swear he'd be perfectly happy if I never got married or had children. That way, I'd never have any distractions from the shop."

"Did you ever think about doing something else?"

She frowned thoughtfully. "I always thought I'd like to be a nurse or even a nurse's aide and work in a doctor's office, but it wasn't in the cards for me."

"That's an admirable profession. You're still young, you could go to school and make that happen. Maybe your dad would initially be unhappy with you, but I'm sure he'd eventually get over it."

"Maybe," she replied, although her tone held no real conviction. "In any case, this morning you get your first exploration of the famous Peterson Pawn shop."

"I'm definitely looking forward to it." He liked it when he could make her smile. Her lovely face was meant for smiling. "Still, you would make a great nurse."

"You really think so?" Her smile widened and her cheeks flushed a pretty pink.

"Definitely. You have a calm, easy way about you that most patients would welcome." It was true. Despite everything that had happened to her, she had a softness that was appealing.

Her cheeks grew an even deeper dusty shade of pink. "Thank you. And now I'd better finish this coffee and head back upstairs to get ready for work."

At eight thirty they left the house. Julie had exchanged her robe for a pair of black slacks and a black T-shirt with Peterson Pawn in bold white letters across her chest. On her feet were black-and-white sandals that exposed her pink-painted toenails.

"Are there other employees besides the family members?" he asked as they left the cul-de-sac.

"A few, although Dad doesn't trust any of them and always thinks they're either stealing items or skimming money from the registers."

"Are they?"

"Not that I'm aware of. I keep the books and there's nothing that would make me think anything improper is happening." She gave a dry laugh. "At least, that's the way I remember things."

"No more flashes of memory since yesterday?" He cast her a quick glance. The morning sunshine loved her features, casting them in a golden glow.

"None." She sighed. "I don't know why I'm so nervous about going back to work."

"Julie, you're missing a lot of memories. I'd expect you to be nervous about anything and everything," he replied. "And you did say that in that flash of memory you were in the pawn shop and you were afraid."

"I'm not even sure if that was a real memory or just some sort of strange anxiety about going back to work." She released another deep sigh.

Before he could stop himself he reached over and touched the back of her hand. "Everything is going to be okay, Julie."

He quickly drew his hand back. He shouldn't touch her. Her skin was so soft and warm, and he liked touching her way too much.

He had to stay focused on the truth of the situation. He'd told her everything would be okay and it would be as long as she didn't regain her memories and nobody killed her for "telling." Everything would be fine as long as no witness could positively identify him and he managed to forget the horrifying vision of McDowell's bloody dead body.

"WELCOME TO MY WORLD," Julie said as she unlocked the front door and led Nick inside the pawn shop. Directly to the left of the door stood a life-size suit of armor and on the right was a full-size skeleton holding a sign that read Shoplifters Will Be Prosecuted.

"Quite a welcoming committee," he replied with a laugh.

She relocked the door behind them. "I told you my father likes a little bizarre with the usual pawn items."

The faint simmer of fear was back inside her. Was it because she was missing her memories or due to something else? She couldn't know. She turned on the lights to further aid the sunshine that danced through the large front windows.

To the left were shelves of computers, monitors and televisions. To the right, musical equipment was on display for purchase. In between were the oversize items for sale. There were lawn mowers and leaf blowers, compressors and all kinds of tools.

Along the back wall stood glass jewelry display cases and the registers. Behind those was a glass-enclosed office and a back room where the customers weren't allowed.

"It's pretty much the way I always thought

a pawn shop would look, just a lot bigger," Nick said.

"Wait...you haven't seen the other room yet." She tried to shove away the niggling sense of anxiety that had been with her since she'd dressed for work that morning.

She watched Nick's expression as she led him into the connecting room. Stunned surprise lit his features just before he released a pleasant rumble of laughter.

"This looks more like Ripley's Believe It or Not! than a pawn shop," he exclaimed.

She gazed around, seeking any changes that might have happened over the last ten months that she couldn't remember. The stuffed, five-legged calf was still there. As were the fat, seven-foot, resin genie seated on a pillow and an equally large, smiling penguin with a belly that opened and closed.

There was also the half dozen antique slot and pinball machines and the unusual artwork hanging on the walls.

Nick walked over to a plaster pink-and-white giraffe and then turned back to look at her. "Where does your father find these things?"

"He doesn't. They mostly find him. Once word got out that he was open to buying and selling almost anything, people started contacting him about unusual items. Come on and I'll show you the office." Her nerves slowly began to calm as she realized nothing much had changed in the shop.

The office was right next to an outer door in the back room, which held various items on shelving. "All the stuff up front is for sale and the things back here are being held for people to reclaim after they've pawned them," she explained. "We also own the building next door that we use to hold all of our pawned things."

"Quite a large operation." Nick looked at her for a long moment. "Are you feeling better about being here?"

"Somewhat better." She smiled. "I'm sure as the day goes on, the last of my nerves will completely disappear."

Still, even just saying those words, she jumped at the sound of the front door opening.

"Hello?" a familiar deep voice called out.

Julie instantly relaxed. "Joel."

She greeted the big, burly man with the slightly shaggy brown hair who would share the workload with her that day. "I'd like you to meet my fiancé," she said.

"Your daddy told me you got a touch of some crazy amnesia, but he didn't mention anything about you getting a fiancé." He smiled at Nick and offered his hand for a shake. "Hope you intend to take good care of this lady," he added after the two men had shaken hands.

"I do," Nick replied.

"She's one fine woman and deserves only the best," Joel replied with a warm smile at her.

"And I have the best," she said with conviction. "Nick, if you want to, you can head on out. It's almost time to open the front doors and I'll be fine here with Joel," she said.

"Walk me to the door?" he asked.

She smiled. "Of course."

"Nice meeting you, Nick," Joel said as they headed for the front door.

"Are you sure you're going to be okay?" Nick asked when they reached the door and the two of them stepped just outside.

"I'll be fine. Joel and I have always been great working buddies," she replied. She frowned. "Unless something happened between us that I don't remember. But everything seemed okay when he came in."

"I thought maybe I'd pick up a couple of

chicken breasts to grill tonight when you get home. I figured we should enjoy the slightly cooler temperatures and the deck while we can."

"Sounds perfect to me." Although most of that crazy simmering fear had eased, there was still a little bit left.

"You know, if you really aren't feeling up to this today, I'll take you right back home."

She shook her head, touched and pleased that he seemed to read all the nuances of her emotions. "I'll be fine...really."

"Then I'll be back here at five to pick you up." He leaned forward and kissed her forehead. "Have a good day, Julie, and call me if you need anything."

Before she could reply...before she could even process the gift of his warm lips against her skin, he turned and was gone.

"Should I go ahead and open the door for the day?" she called to Joel, who had taken a position behind the counter.

"I'm ready if you are."

She unlocked the door and her official day at work began. It was a busy morning with people coming in to shop or to pawn. Julie scarcely had any time to think about any lingering fear that might attempt to possess her.

Her missing memories didn't hinder her as the day went on. It was two o'clock and in the middle of a lull when a middle-aged woman came in. She walked hesitantly up to the counter, tightly clutching a worn purse in both hands.

"May I help you?" Julie asked.

"Uh… I don't know." The woman shoved a strand of her long brown hair behind one ear. "I've never done this before, but I guess I'd like to pawn a ring."

"May I see the ring?"

She placed her purse on the counter, opened it and withdrew a small envelope. Her fingers trembled as she shook out a small diamond ring.

Julie grabbed a jeweler's loop and looked at the ring carefully. It was only fourteen karat gold and the diamond was tiny, although had fairly good clarity. She looked back at the woman. "I can do a hundred dollars," she offered.

"That's all? It's my wedding ring and I promise I'll be back to get it, but I need a hundred and thirty dollars to pay for our electric bill. I spent too much on groceries and now I'm in a bind." She laughed, although it was a desperate sound. "But I'm sure you hear sob stories all the time."

Julie had definitely heard a lot of sob stories over the years, but something about this woman touched her heart. "I'll give you a hundred and forty dollars."

Tears suddenly misted the woman's eyes. "Oh…thank you. And this will be a secret, right. I mean nobody else will have to know that I've pawned it."

"Nobody will know unless you tell them," Julie replied. *Don't tell.* The words thundered in her head as she scanned Maggie Albright's driver's license. The two words resounded over and over again as she explained the terms and conditions of the pawn.

Had something happened here in the pawn shop that had prompted the threat to her? Why couldn't she remember? Had a customer somehow forced her to do something illegal? She couldn't imagine that being the case. She had always played by the rules but, without her memory, she couldn't fully dismiss such a scenario, either.

At three, Casey called to tell Julie she was running late and couldn't make it in to relieve her until six thirty or so. Julie called Nick so he would know to come later to pick her up.

"If that girl ever shows up on time for one of her shifts, I'll swallow my tongue," Joel said drily.

Julie laughed. "Nobody ever said Casey was dependable. Beautiful, yes. Fun, definitely. Her idea of responsibility is if she remembers to call in and let us know she's going to be late or not show up at all."

"I heard through the grapevine that your dad had a talk with her and told her it was time for her to grow up and pay her own bills."

She looked at Joel in surprise. "Now, that I haven't heard."

Joel released a small burst of laughter. "I'm not sure Casey believed him because she sure hasn't been too eager to pick up extra shifts."

"I doubt if the talk worried her much. She's always had my parents wrapped around her little finger," Julie replied.

She began to relax again as she and Joel talked shop and he regaled her with stories about his new puppy named Buster.

"Have you told me about Buster before?" she asked.

He smiled at her kindly. "Two weeks ago when I first got the pooch. It's okay, Julie. I know you're missing some memories right now. I can't imagine what that's like."

"Unsettling and more than a little bit frightening. I'm just hoping before too long everything will come back to me. In fact, while nobody is in here, I'd like to go back into the office and read over the transactions from the last day I worked. Maybe that will help jog my memory."

"Knock yourself out," Joel replied. "It's really slow right now and, if I need you, I'll holler for you. Julie, if there was something I could do to help, you know I'd do it."

"Thanks, Joel." She gave him a grateful smile and then hurried into the office space and sat at the desk. According to the schedule posted on the wall, she'd worked the day before her car accident.

She pulled out the paperwork and pored over the transactions she'd been in charge of that day, trying to find something—anything—that would have to do with a deadly secret.

There had to be something to explain that terrible phone call she'd received and she needed to find out what it was sooner rather than later.

Chapter Six

"I went over all the transactions for the entire week before my accident and I didn't find anything suspicious," she told Nick when they were in his car and heading home.

"Then maybe whatever it is doesn't have anything to do with the pawn shop." He turned into the cul-de-sac.

"Maybe. But I had that faint sense of fear all day long while I was there, and I didn't have much of a life outside the pawn shop until you came along."

"But hasn't that fear been with you since you woke up in the hospital?" He parked the car and turned off the engine.

"I guess," she conceded. They got out of the car and walked to the front door. She didn't know how to explain to him that she had two different feelings of fear. One definitely came from her missing time with the amnesia. The other was more insidious...a sick anxiety that kept her on edge.

"Go straight to the deck and have a seat," he instructed her once they were inside. "I've got dinner covered."

"Are you sure?" she asked in surprise.

"Positive. Would you like a beer?"

"I think I have some white wine in the fridge. I'd love a glass of that," she replied.

"Done. Now go relax," he commanded.

"Yes, sir," she replied with a laugh. She stepped outside and was surprised to see the table already set. She sank down into one of the cushioned chairs and kicked off her sandals. It was after seven and she was exhausted.

"Here we go." Nick came out of the door with a glass of wine in one hand and two chicken breasts on a plate, seasoned and ready to go on the grill, in the other.

"Thanks." She took the glass from him and watched as he fired up the barbecue and then placed the chicken breasts on the rack.

Dark clouds had appeared in the sky over the course of the long day. "Is it supposed to rain?" she asked.

"There's a possibility of some storms in

the area later this evening," he replied and sat across from her.

"The grass could definitely use the rain, but I absolutely hate thunder and lightning."

He grinned at her, a light, easy gesture that warmed her more than the sultry evening air could ever do. "So, you're a big 'fraidy cat and hide under the sheets when it storms?"

"Something like that. And over the past ten months, were there times when you hid under the sheets with me?"

"Once or twice." He jumped up from the chair and went to the grill to check on the chicken.

She took a sip of her wine and released a sigh. She missed the intimacy she and Nick must have had. She missed it even though she didn't remember it. And she desperately wanted to remember him. She needed to remember them.

She closed her eyes and instantly a vision filled her head. She was at the pawn shop and a man was yelling at her. His face was red with anger and he pounded a fist on the counter. She knew he was yelling at her because his mouth was moving, but she couldn't hear him.

The stranger's face melted and transformed

into her brother Max's face. He was shouting at her, too. Angry. Her stomach clenched. An icy fist grabbed her throat. She couldn't breathe.

A hand fell on her shoulder and she jerked rigid with fear. Her eyes flipped open. Nick gazed at her with concern. "Are you all right?" he asked worriedly. "You disappeared there for a minute."

"A memory." She cleared her throat and swallowed against the thick fear that attempted to rise up. "At least, I think it was a memory."

"Want to talk about it?" He sat on the chair closest to her and took her hand in his.

She welcomed the warmth of his hand around hers as she told him where her mind had taken her. "We sometimes get customers who had lost their item due to non-payment and they often get very angry. As far as Max yelling at me…he yells at everyone, so that's nothing new." She frowned thoughtfully. "I don't know if any of it means something or if it all means nothing."

"I would imagine your memory is going to return in bits and pieces that might not make sense right now." He squeezed her hand. "Eventually it will all come back and everything will make sense." He stood and walked back to the barbecue where he turned the chicken breasts.

Dinner was pleasant and they lingered on the deck until lightning began to slash across the night sky and they had to move inside.

Nick insisted on doing the kitchen cleanup and she sat at the table while he worked. "So, how did you spend the day?" she asked.

"I immersed myself in football. I watched DVDs from last year's games and tried to identify the strengths and weaknesses of my players."

"Do you love what you do?" she asked curiously.

He turned from the sink. "I do."

"Did you want to be a professional football player?"

He shook his head. "No way. I always wanted to be a coach. I love the game and I love the kids."

"Did we talk about having children?" How she wished she could remember every conversation they'd ever had.

"Not really, although I assumed you wanted them."

"I do. I'd like to have at least a boy and a girl. What about you?"

"That works for me," he replied. He finished up with the dishes and joined her at the kitchen table.

"Now, do you work again tomorrow?" he asked.

"I'm on the schedule for early shifts for the next four days," she replied. "And then I go to afternoon shifts for a few days."

"When is your day off?"

She frowned. "We rarely get days off."

"You're kidding. That isn't right. Everyone deserves a day off." He looked down at the table for a moment and then gazed back at her. "I don't want to make you angry, but don't you think it's maybe possible your family is taking advantage of you?"

She started to protest but instead nodded slowly in agreement. "I know they are. It's the way things have always been. I not only work long hours in the store, but I also keep track of the inventory, keep the financial records and do the taxes every year."

"Maybe it's time to change things up. Otherwise your obligations to them will choke any hope you have of being a wife and having children. You deserve more, Julie." He rose. "And now, I think it's time we both get a good night's sleep."

Within minutes she was upstairs in her room. Nick's words still echoed in her head as she changed into a short pink nightgown. Was it possible she'd mentioned to Max that she wanted a day off? Shorter hours? And had that been the memory she'd had of Max raging at her?

She believed she'd known for a long time that she wasn't particularly happy working long hours at the shop. Nick was right, she deserved more than a pawn shop in her life. She wanted a husband and children, and she wanted time to make those things happen.

She probably would have brought it up with her brother before speaking to her father about it. She could see herself torn between the family business and time with Nick. Had she rocked the boat and asked for less responsibility?

With Nick in her life, she imagined her priorities might have changed. Maybe she'd wanted to go to one of his football games or to spend more than one night a week with him. Had she voiced her desire to stop working so much and gained Max's anger? Still, none of that answered what she might know that she wasn't supposed to tell.

She jumped as a rumble of thunder boomed.

Terrific, she thought. Just what she needed on top of everything else. She'd been afraid of thunderstorms for as long as she could remember. Logically she knew they couldn't hurt her, but that logic went out the window when it thundered. She also knew she was a baby when it came to storms, but even that didn't help.

She was about to get into bed when she remembered her sandals beneath the table on the deck. They were one of her favorite pairs and they were part fabric. The rain would probably ruin them.

With a sigh of resignation she stepped out of her bedroom. The hallway was dark, as was Nick's room down the hall. He'd probably already fallen asleep.

Silently, and in the dark, she crept past his doorway and down the stairs. Despite her lack of certain memories, she knew her surroundings intimately. She walked through the living room and into the kitchen to get to the patio door.

She'd just reached it when lightning flashed, half blinding her yet leaving her with enough sight to see somebody—some…thing—in the door window.

She froze. Terror gripped her. A roll of

thunder shook the house and still she remained unmoving. Lightning once again flashed and this time she saw a face—a face with no eyes. What? Who?

Her brain went numb even as she stumbled backward from the horrific sight. Finally she managed to scream.

THE SCREAM PENETRATED Nick's sleep and bolted him upright in bed. Julie! He pulled on a pair of shorts and shot down the hallway to her room.

She screamed again and he realized she was someplace downstairs. He flipped on the hall light, his heart beating wildly as a surge of adrenaline had him taking the stairs two at a time.

He also turned on the living room light and then he saw her. She stood in a pink nightgown just inside the kitchen and her facial features were twisted in sheer terror.

"Julie! What is it?" He raced to her side, wondering what was happening. What was she doing down here? Had it been the thunder or the lightning that had her so upset? Had she suffered a nightmare? A frightening memory?

She raised a trembling hand and pointed

to the back door. Nick turned and looked and jumped in surprise. What in the hell? A doll. It hung from the doorframe and might have stared inside if its eyes hadn't been gouged out.

He turned on the kitchen light. "It's okay, Julie. It's a doll. It can't hurt you." As she stumbled to the table and sank down in a chair, he opened the back door and grabbed the offending doll. It had been hung by a piece of thick string that easily gave way when he pulled on it.

It was monstrous. Along with the missing eyes, the hair had been pulled out and a small knife had been driven to its hilt into the soft skull. Across the bare belly the words *Don't Tell* had been written in a red marker.

"It's just a doll," he repeated.

Julie raised her eyes from the doll to him. Her face was deathly pale and her lips trembled. "Who is doing this?" Her dark blue eyes held a wealth of fear. "This is monstrous. This is…is so evil. Who…who would do such a thing to me?"

Nick grabbed a towel off the countertop and tossed it over the doll on the table. "I don't know, but I think it's time we call the police." The very last thing he wanted was any contact with the law, but he couldn't leave Julie at risk to save himself.

The danger the phone call had yielded had suddenly escalated with this gruesome find. Even worse, whoever had done this knew exactly where she lived, had actually been on her back deck.

"I'm just not sure what the police can do about any of this," she finally replied. A boom of thunder shook the house and increased the panic in her eyes.

"Julie, we still need to call them and make a record of this. I'll go upstairs and grab my cell phone and be right back down."

"I'm coming with you." She jumped up from the chair like an uncoordinated colt, her knees buckling beneath her.

He grabbed her, afraid she might fall to the floor.

Instantly she wrapped her arms around his neck and began to weep. Her slender body trembled against his and he fully embraced her, knowing it was sheer terror that caused her tears. Certainly the doll had more than unsettled him. He wasn't sure whose heart beat faster, hers or his own. Who was doing this to her and why? And what might the next move be? How much danger was she really in?

He caressed her back and tried to ignore the press of her breasts against him and the dizzying scent of her that wrapped around him. "Come on, Julie. Let's go make that phone call."

She released her hold on him and he grabbed her hand. She held tight, radiating her fear in the iciness of her fingers as they headed up the stairs.

The storm was upon them with rain slashing at the windows and continuous lightning and thunder. She clung so close to his side it made their trek upstairs an awkward dance.

When they reached his room, she sat on the edge of the bed while he called the police. "They should be here in just a few minutes," he said, hanging up. "Let's go back downstairs to wait for them."

Before heading downstairs they went to her bedroom, where she grabbed a robe to pull on around her nightgown.

Back in the living room, she curled up into a corner of the sofa, her face still far too pale and her eyes silently screaming with her fear.

He wanted to take that emotion out of her eyes. He never wanted to hear her scream like she had again. But at this moment he couldn't even assure her that everything was going to be okay because he didn't know what might happen next.

"I saw some tea bags up in the cupboard. Do you want me to make you a cup of hot tea while we wait?" he asked.

She looked so cold with her arms wrapped tightly around her, as if the fear inside her had stolen every ounce of her body heat.

"That would be nice. There's a teakettle in the cabinet under the coffeemaker." Her voice was higher than usual and her lips trembled.

He had just put the water on to boil when a knock fell on the front door. As he walked through the living room to answer it, he hoped like hell all the cops in Kansas City law enforcement didn't have a sketch of him as a person of interest in the murder.

He opened the door and two officers flashed their badges and swept inside, their rain hats and suits dripping water on the floor. "Sorry," the taller of the two said. "It's a heck of a rainstorm out there."

"No problem," Nick replied. "Why don't I take your coats and hang them?" There was a three-hook coat hanger just inside the front door.

Introductions weren't officially made until their coats were off and they'd all stepped into the living room where Julie hadn't moved from her position on the sofa.

Officer Sean White and Officer Frank Roberts stood while Nick explained why they had been called out on a stormy night. As he told them about the phone call and then the doll, Officer Roberts's dark eyes gazed at him intently.

Paranoia immediately filled Nick. Did the officer know something about McDowell's murder? Was it suspicion that had the man staring at Nick so attentively?

A shrill whistle filled the air. Julie released a small scream and the two officers went for their guns. "It's the teakettle," Nick said hurriedly. "If you'll follow me into the kitchen, I'll show you the doll."

In the kitchen he quickly pulled the kettle off the burner, stopping its noisy hiss, and then took the towel off the doll.

"Now that's a nasty piece of work," Officer White said in obvious disgust.

"I hope you're going to take it away." Julie spoke from the doorway.

"And you don't have any idea what this is all about?" Officer White asked her.

Julie shook her head. "I… I had a car accident a couple of days ago and it's done something to some of my memories."

"You said the threatening phone call came from an anonymous number?" he continued.

She nodded.

"Probably a burner phone," Officer Roberts said. He turned his gaze back to Nick. "Can you think of anyone who might want to harm Ms. Peterson?"

Despite the coolness of the house, Nick felt warm…too warm. Why was the officer looking at him with such scrutiny?

"No, nobody," he replied.

"You're Coach Simon, aren't you?" Roberts suddenly asked. Nick nodded and the officer elaborated. "I knew I'd seen you before. My boy played for you a couple of years ago… Cody Roberts?"

Nick breathed a sigh of relief. "Sure, I remember Cody. He was a good tight end. Is he still at KU?"

"Yeah, but he's not playing football anymore. He's pretty focused on his classes. He wants to get a degree in criminology. Seems he wants to follow in his old man's footsteps." Roberts's broad chest puffed up.

"Enough about football and kids," Officer

White said. "We need to get moving before the next wave of storms moves in."

Nick suddenly realized the thunder and lightning had abated and the rain had stopped. "There are more storms moving in?" Julie asked half breathlessly.

"The weather reports are for bands to continue to move in and out until dawn," Officer White replied. "We'll take the doll with us and attempt to pull off some fingerprints, but don't expect too much."

"This might be nothing more than scare tactics, but I'd say the best thing you can do is try to think of anyone who might have a beef with you." Roberts pulled on a pair of gloves, took a large plastic bag out of his back pocket and bagged the offending toy.

All of them walked to the front door.

Officer White took a card out of his pocket and offered it to Julie. "You call me if you think of anyone or if anything else happens. In the meantime, I'll open a file and if we get anything at all off the doll then I'll contact you."

"Thank you," she replied.

Within minutes the officers had pulled on their rain gear and left. Nick locked up after them and then turned to look at Julie. "Still want that cup of tea? I can reheat the water."

She stared at him, her eyes filled with fear and quiet despair. "I'm frightened and I've never been so cold in my life. I don't want hot tea. I want you. I want you to hold me through the night. I need you, Nick, and if you really love me, you'll sleep with me tonight."

Chapter Seven

Her hair smelled of peaches as stray strands tickled the side of his face. He had one arm around her and she fit perfectly against him, curled up at his side as he lay on his back.

He'd had no choice but to climb into her bed. It would have been odd for a fiancé not to hold the woman he professed to love through a dark and stormy night and after she'd had such a bad scare.

Thankfully, almost the minute they had gotten comfortable in the bed, she had fallen asleep. Sleep was the last thing on his mind. If her warm, curvy body next to his wasn't enough of a distraction, his racing thoughts kept sleep at bay.

What he wanted to stay focused on was the question of who was threatening Julie and not on the white-hot desire that pulsed in his veins.

Was it possible it was somebody in her family? None of them seemed the type to issue anonymous warnings. They were more up-front and in-your-face. Was it somebody who worked with her at the pawn shop?

Unfortunately he had the feeling that the police would be little help in solving this mystery. They had much bigger crimes to solve—like the vicious murder of Brian McDowell. And crime certainly hadn't stopped with that murder.

His stomach clenched tight as he thought of how uncomfortable he'd been when Officer Roberts had eyed him so closely. Guilt had coalesced with paranoia and he'd been certain the night would end with him under arrest. How did real criminals live with that?

A faint flash of lightning lit the room, followed several moments later by a rumble of thunder. Thankfully, Julie didn't stir.

He didn't want her awake. Being next to her as she slept was difficult enough. He hadn't felt this kind of desire for a woman since Debbie. After her death, he'd believed he'd never want a woman again. But Julie definitely stirred that emotion inside him.

It wasn't just about feeling the softness of her skin next to his. It was far more than the heady scent of her. Her warm smile made him want her. Her laughter pulled him to her.

There had been so very little laughter in his life over the past three years. There had been very little life. He'd been dead inside since he'd buried his wife and Julie reminded him that there was still life and laughter and desire.

Not that it mattered. He wasn't in the market for a wife. And, in any case, he had damned any future relationship with Julie the minute he'd told his first lie to her. What he didn't understand was why this thought depressed him more than a little bit.

He must have dozed off because he suddenly jerked awake. Had the thunder awakened him? Perhaps. As he remained still, a bright flash lit the room and thunder boomed overhead.

Beside him, Julie moaned. "No." She punched at the sheet that covered them and thrashed around. "No. Go away." Her voice held a desperate appeal. "Go away!" She sat upright, her chest heaving and her eyes wild as lightning flashed again.

"Julie." He sat up beside her and reached over to turn on the bedside lamp. The pupils of her eyes were dilated, nearly usurping all their blue color. He said her name once again. She stared at him for a long moment and then released a startled gasp.

"I'm sorry. I'm so sorry. It was a nightmare." She drew her knees up to her chest as if attempting to disappear. "I didn't mean to wake you."

"Was it the storm?" he asked.

"No…it was the doll." She raised a hand to the bottom of her throat, a gesture he had come to recognize as a display of her anxiety. "I dreamed it was alive and it was trying to come into the house to kill me." She lowered her legs and turned toward him. "Nick, I'm so sorry I disturbed your sleep."

"Don't apologize for a bad dream," he replied. "We all have them at one time or another."

She rolled over so her upper body was on top of his bare chest. All his muscles tensed and he closed his eyes as a fiery desire coursed through him. She swept a hand across his skin and whispered a sigh against his neck.

He wanted to douse the flames she stirred inside him, but as she moved her hand lower on his abdomen, the flames only burned hotter.

"Nick," she said softly as her fingers toyed with the waistband of his boxers.

He opened his eyes and her lips were right next to his. Her eyes telegraphed need and want. With a groan, he pulled her closer against him as his lips captured hers.

Someplace in the back of his mind he knew this was wrong on so many levels. But that didn't stop him from rolling her over onto her back and continuing to kiss her. Rationality certainly didn't halt his hands that found her soft breasts and taut nipples.

He was going to make love to her. She'd believe she was making love with a man who loved her, who had committed his life to her. She wouldn't know yet that he was nothing more than a virtual stranger to her. Even with all that in his head, it wasn't enough to stop the moment.

Their tongues swirled together with a frantic hunger. She tasted of hot desire and he loved the taste of her as they continued the kiss.

He stroked his hands across her shoulders and down her arms. Her warm and silky skin was made for a man's caress. She moaned slightly against his mouth. The husky sound, so filled with her desire for him, heated the blood flowing through his veins.

He was half breathless and yet he didn't want to stop tasting her sweet lips. When thunder boomed overhead, she didn't flinch. It was as if she was completely lost in him. And that only turned him on more.

She finally stopped, only to sit up and shrug the spaghetti straps of her nightgown off her shoulders. The silky garment fell to her waist. The sight of her breasts in the flashing lightning coming through the window made him want to touch.

He covered her breasts with his hands, loving the feel of softness and the pebble hardness of her nipples. He moved his lips to cover where his hands had been.

"Oh, Nick," she whispered and placed her hands on the back of his head to encourage the intimacy.

As the storm raged outside, the rest of their clothes were abandoned. She was beautiful in her clothes, but she was breathtakingly beautiful naked.

She showed no shyness or hesitation. Rather, she was passionate and exciting. She had no idea this was the first time they had ever made love. She met him with the confidence of a long-time lover and a woman who was certain she was loved.

For every caress he gave her, she gave back to him until he had to take her completely. Anything less was impossible.

He hovered between her thighs. He gazed down at her. Her pupils were still wide, but he knew now it was from desire and not any fear.

"Take me, Nick," she said, her voice husky with desire. "I want you so badly."

"And I want you." He eased into her and was immediately lost in her heat. She met him thrust for thrust, moaning her pleasure as her fingers clutched at his back.

Too fast. Everything was happening too fast and he tried to slow down. He wanted her with him when he reached his peak. He wanted to make sure she was thoroughly pleasured before he allowed himself his own.

And then she was there, her body tensing as she moaned again and again. Small shudders swept through her and his release was upon him. Intense...wild, his climax rocketed through him.

He finally collapsed onto his elbows, keeping the bulk of his weight off her. She looked stunning with her dark hair splayed out on the pillow and her cheeks flushed with color.

She reached up, placed her hands on either side of his face and then rose just enough to meet her lips with his. He tasted her love in the softness of the kiss. A love she'd given to him without question, without any reservation.

"That was magic," she said when the kiss ended.

"Yeah, it was."

"Has it always been that good?"

"Always." He got up from the bed, grabbed his boxers from the floor and went down the hallway to the bathroom he'd been using. He didn't want to linger and give her an opportunity to say anything more about what they'd just shared. He didn't want to utter one more lie to her tonight.

He looked at his reflection in the mirror with disgust. This was the absolute worst thing he could have done to her. Hell, he hadn't even used a condom. He'd been so caught up in the haze of desire, he hadn't thought about protection.

When her memories came back to her, there would be no way to protect her from knowing he wasn't who he claimed to be. He'd taken advantage of her in so many ways and tonight in the worst way possible. He was a fraud pretending to be a fiancé for his own selfish purposes.

A boom of thunder sounded overhead.

Run, a little voice whispered in his head. *Get your things and get out of here now.*

"I can't," he said to the man in the mirror.

He was in way too deep now. Not only was he afraid for her, he'd also grown to care about her. He couldn't just run away like a coward, especially after what they'd just shared.

This whole ordeal had started because of his hatred, because of his rage toward another man. But now it was so much more complicated than that. At the moment that particular rage seemed distant and rather unimportant.

Pulling his boxers back on, he knew exactly what he was going to do now. He was going to return to her bed and hold her. He was going to continue to hold her until the thunder and lightning stopped because he knew she was afraid of those things.

He left the bathroom and went into the bedroom, where she was just getting back into bed. She smiled at him, but the smile was short-lived as thunder once again boomed.

"Let's cover up our heads," he said, hoping to keep things light between them despite what had just happened. Besides, the last thing he wanted was a recap of their love-making where she told him how very much she loved him.

"Sounds good to me," she replied.

Minutes later the light on the nightstand had been turned off and he was spooned around her back. Her body tensed slightly each time the storm made its presence known.

"I don't know why I'm such a baby," she said softly.

"Everyone has an irrational fear about something," he replied.

"What's yours?" she asked drowsily.

He couldn't tell her that his biggest fear at the moment was being arrested for murder. Or that his second biggest fear was what would happen when she regained her memories.

"Nick? Are you asleep?"

He didn't reply.

Within minutes her breathing became the slow and regular rhythm of sleep.

Sleep didn't come so easily to him.

He should be arrested. He should spend the rest of his life in a jail cell. His crimes against Julie would haunt him for the rest of his life. And tonight he'd committed the worst kind of felony against her by making love to her.

He needed to find out who was threatening her. He didn't want her to face whatever danger might be reaching out for her all alone. Once that mystery was solved, whether she had her memories back or not, he had to tell her the truth. He had to let her know that he wasn't her fiancé and he'd lied about everything.

He just couldn't figure out why his heart ached just a little even thinking about it.

JULIE WOKE ALONE in the bed with bright morning sunshine drifting through the curtains. She moved a hand to Nick's side of the bed and the warmth that lingered there let her know he'd gotten up only recently. The sheets still held the faint aroma of his cologne.

She closed her eyes and released a sigh of utter contentment. Making love with him had been wonderful. It had been everything she'd imagined it would be. He'd been so passionate and yet tender, and sleeping in his arms had felt like home.

She was almost sorry he was already out of bed. She wouldn't have minded a repeat performance. "You're going to have the rest of your life with him," she whispered to her pillow. The words warmed her. He was everything she wanted for herself. She just wished she could remember all the moments she'd spent with him before now.

Remember. The threatening phone call… the horrific doll… She so desperately needed to remember so she'd know where those threats were coming from. Who was responsible? She squeezed her eyes more tightly closed, trying to summon something—anything—from her not-so-distant past.

There was nothing there. It was like a big black hole that swirled and whirled inside her head but gave up nothing.

With a frustrated sigh, she got out of bed.

Pulling a short, cotton robe around her, she went into the bathroom to brush her teeth and hair before joining her fiancé for morning coffee.

Her fiancé… Her heart thrilled.

Thank goodness he'd gotten over his reticence to make love to her and now they could truly enjoy the intimacy of a couple in love.

She wore a smile as she left the bedroom and headed down the stairs. She found Nick exactly where she expected him to be, at the kitchen table with a cup of coffee and the morning paper before him.

"Good morning." The words nearly sang

out of her before she dropped a kiss on his forehead. She felt so much closer to him since last night.

"Somebody is in a good mood," he said.

She walked over to the counter and then turned to face him. "And why shouldn't I be? Fresh coffee is waiting for me, the storms have passed and I have the hottest fiancé in the world right here with me."

"And he's about to burst your bubble of happiness," he replied. "Grab your coffee and then I want to have a serious talk with you."

Her heart plummeted as she turned around to pour her coffee. Had last night's lovemaking made him suddenly decide he didn't love her anymore? Were her amnesia and the threats all too much for him to deal with? Was he about to break her heart? Oh, God, she hoped not.

She joined him at the table, her heart trembling with dread as she gazed into his dark-lashed green eyes.

"I've been thinking about the threats you've received and I think maybe you and I need to get more proactive."

A huge relief swept through her. At least he hadn't been thinking about leaving her. "Proactive how?"

"You need a security system and I'd like to get one installed here today while you're at work."

She sat back in the chair and looked at him in surprise.

"Julie, whoever is threatening you knows where you live. Somebody was on your deck last night. They could have easily gained entry into the house. We have to take this seriously."

"And you don't think the police will be able to get anything off the doll?" The icy chill from the night before threatened to overtake her once again. She wrapped her fingers around her coffee cup in an effort to get warm again.

"I think it's highly doubtful. I also want you to make a list of everyone who works at the pawn shop with you."

"I can do that, but what do you intend to do with the information?" She took a sip of coffee and eyed him over the rim of the cup.

"I'm going to play at being an amateur detective. At the very least, I can check out their social media and see if anything pops up that might give you a clue as to who is doing this and why."

"So, should I start calling you Sherlock?"

She attempted to put a little levity into the situation to ward off the inner chill that threatened.

He flashed a grin. "As long as I get to be Sherlock without the silly hat and the pipe." His smile faded. "Seriously, Julie, what do you say about getting the security system done today? I'll take care of all the details and will be here for it to be installed."

In an instant a hundred what-ifs went through her head. What if the person hadn't just stopped at the back door to hang a doll, but had broken the window and gotten into the house? With the rumbles of the storm overhead, she and Nick probably wouldn't have known that anyone was inside.

Somebody could have easily crept up the stairs and entered her bedroom. Who knew what could have happened.

"Yes, it's a good idea, and I'd like it done as soon as possible," she replied. She took another sip of her coffee, hoping the warm liquid could heat the cold places inside her their conversation had created. "I'll make that list for you right now."

She got up from the table and went to the built-in desk in the corner of the kitchen. She opened one of the drawers and pulled out a pad of paper and a pen. She then returned to the table and began to list the names of the employees of the pawn shop.

As she wrote down each name, she couldn't help but wonder… *Is this person terrorizing me? Is he or she wanting to harm me? What secret was worth all this?*

"Don't you have any friends? In all the time I've known you, you've never mentioned any personal friends." She looked up to see Nick eyeing her curiously.

She frowned thoughtfully. "I've never really had time for friends. My mother and Casey are pretty much the only friends I've had. The three of us usually manage to go out about once a month or so for dinner and drinks. Why did you ask?"

"I just wondered if there was anyone else who needs to be written down on that list. Anyone you have interaction with who would know not only your phone number but also your address."

"Not that I can think of," she replied. "But since I can't remember the last ten months of my life, I guess it's possible there might be somebody."

She held his gaze for a long moment. "What I don't understand is, if I was in some kind of trouble before the accident, why didn't I talk to you about it?"

"Unfortunately, I can't answer that." He got up from the table and poured himself another cup of coffee.

Minutes later, after finishing the list of names Nick had requested, she was in the shower and preparing herself for another day at work. But her conversation with Nick lingered in her head.

She'd never really thought about all she'd sacrificed for the family business. There had been no friends in her life, no giggling girls at a slumber party, no best friend to tell all her secrets to. Casey had been a fun little sister, but a younger sibling wasn't the same as having a best friend.

There had been many sacrifices over the years. Running the family business had never been her dream, it had been her parents' dream for her. But she'd never really considered letting them down by choosing something else.

Nick was right. She was still young. She was only thirty-one. She could go back to school and fulfill her dreams for herself. As she rinsed her hair, she envisioned that future.

She and Nick would be married. She'd maybe get a job in a doctor's office where she could be home every evening with her husband. Eventually they'd have children and she would make sure that they got the childhood she'd never had.

Their children would have sleepovers and best friends and, other than chores, they wouldn't start working when they were eight or ten like she had. Instead their childhoods would be filled with laughter and they would have time to just be kids.

All she had to do to make that dream come true was to tell her parents she wanted out. Even thinking about that difficult conversation made her stomach twist and knot with anxiety.

Had she already told her parents she wanted to make some major changes in her life? Somehow she believed she hadn't told them yet. She didn't believe she would have told them until they'd known about Nick.

Until she had her memories back, she'd keep the status quo. She didn't need the drama that would take place in talking to her parents. She had more than enough drama in her life at the moment.

"WHILE YOU WERE in the shower, I contacted a security company who's coming out here at noon," Nick said when they were in the car and heading to the pawn shop.

"Just tell me what it costs and I'll write you a check."

"We'll worry about that later. The important thing is making sure nobody can breach the security of your home," he replied.

She stared at his profile, noting the strength in his jawline and the straightness of his nose. The familiar scent of his cologne wrapped around her. "I always feel safe when I'm with you."

He flashed her a quick glance. "That's nice, but eventually I'll have to go back to work and we'll be on different schedules. The security system will make me feel better about your safety when I'm not around."

Julie stared out the passenger window, dread rising inside her as she thought of Nick going back to work. Hopefully, by the time that happened, the mystery of the threats against her would be solved. And, hopefully, then the only thing on her mind would be planning a wedding.

"I'll be back here at five to pick you up," Nick said as he pulled up to the pawn shop front door.

"If I'm going to be later than that, I'll call you."

She got out of the car and waved as he pulled away.

The door of the shop was already unlocked. She entered to see her brother, Tony, wiping down the display counter with glass cleaner.

"I thought I was working with Casey today," she said.

"She woke up with a sore throat and called Dad, who then called me to come in to work." Tony smiled at her. "I don't mind so much since this gives us a good opportunity to catch up with each other."

"Sounds good to me," she replied. "Want some help?" She gestured to the rest of the dusty display case.

"Nah, I've got it. Just sit and relax while you have a chance."

She sat on one of the tall stools behind the counter and watched as he got back to work. There was only a year's difference in age between her and Tony and she'd always felt closest to him.

They were both alike in temperament. They were both non-confrontational and more introverted than their older brother and younger sister. They had understood each other and had felt most comfortable in each other's company.

"So, what's new in your life? Has anything happened that I don't remember?" she asked.

He finished up dusting and sat. "Absolutely nothing is new."

"Still no girlfriend?"

"Who has time? Your Nick has to be a real patient guy to have put up with your work schedule for so long," he replied.

They only had a few minutes to visit with each other before people began to come in.

Business was steady until just after noon and then once again she and Tony were alone in the shop.

"Why don't I go into the office and make a fresh pot of coffee?" she suggested.

"Sounds good, and while you do that I'll order us some lunch. How does Chinese sound?"

"Hmm, I'm up for some sweet and sour chicken," she replied. There were half a dozen places that delivered and a good Chinese place down the road was one of them. She slid off the stool and was about to head toward the office when he stopped her.

"Julie, you still really don't remember anything?" he asked.

"A few bits and pieces, but nothing that makes any sense."

"Then you don't remember the conversation we had the last time we worked together."

Julie shook her head. "What conversation did we have?"

Tony shrugged. "It doesn't matter."

"Tony, it must have been important since you asked. I'm not going to make the coffee until you tell me what we talked about."

He gave her a wry grin. "Holding coffee hostage is definitely an effective way to make me talk." His grin faded as he gazed at her soberly. "I told you I'd started taking some online college classes because I want out of here."

Surprise winged through her. "Have you told Mom and Dad?"

"No!" he said sharply. "I'm not ready to tell them yet. The only reason I told you was because you told me you wanted out of here, too."

"I do," she replied. "Although I haven't done anything to advance a move right now. But I know having Nick in my life has made me want a more normal schedule, and we both know I won't get that working here."

He nodded in agreement. "I just wanted

to make sure if you did remember anything about our conversation that you didn't say anything to Mom and Dad."

"Don't worry, I'll keep your secret, Tony," she assured him.

Was this the secret she wasn't supposed to tell? Was it possible her brother had made the phone call and left the doll hanging on her door? No, it couldn't be possible. There was no way she'd believe it had been her brother. Tony wasn't that kind of man. Was he?

"I'll get the coffee going," she said as she consciously pushed thoughts of the threats she'd received away and Tony away.

She was headed for the office where the coffee machine was located when a vision leaped into her head.

She'd left her phone at work. It was midnight when she realized it. In her car and headed to the shop, she was irritated to be out this late. But she needed her phone since she wasn't working tomorrow...

She entered through the back door and walked into the office, lit only with the dim security lights. Her phone sat right where she'd left it in the middle of the desk. She pulled out

the chair, sat and checked to see if any mes-
sages had come in that she needed to address.

As she tapped the button to enter her mes-
sage box, the back door exploded inward.
Instantly she jumped up, her heart pounding
with terror. Was somebody breaking in to rob
the place? On shaky legs, she moved to the
office door and peered out—

THE VISION OR memory or whatever it was
snapped shut in her mind. She found herself leaning weakly against the office door
with the taste of fear lingering heavily in her
mouth.

What had happened that night? Who had
she seen come in the back door? Had the
door been locked or unlocked? She raised her
hands to the sides of her head and pressed
tightly. Why couldn't she remember anything
more?

Had the door been locked or had she left it
unlocked when she'd gone into the office? It
was an important question that went around
and around in her head. If she'd locked the
door, then it had been unlocked by a family
member or an employee who had the key. If
she'd left it unlocked, then any stranger off
the street could have come inside.

Something bad had happened that night. She felt the rightness of her thought. It had been something so terrible that her brain was now trying to protect her by not allowing her to remember it. Had she been attacked? Dear God, had she been raped?

Don't tell. The words thundered through her brain and she squeezed her hands more tightly against the sides of her head. Was it possible somebody who worked here, somebody she had trusted, had attacked her and then threatened her not to tell?

Chapter Eight

"I'm sure something happened at the shop,"
Julie said as Nick drove her home after work.
She shared with him the memory she'd had.
"It was something bad. I think it was some-
thing terrible."

Nick glanced at her. She wore her anxiety
in the tiny wrinkle across her forehead and
in the way one of her hands moved against
the bottom of her throat, as if she was having
trouble swallowing.

"There is a bit of good news in all this,"
he said.

She eyed him in disbelief. "And what
would that possibly be?"

"Whatever bad thing might have happened
at the pawn shop, you survived it."

She appeared to visibly relax. "Thank you
for reminding me of that."

"On another positive note, your new alarm

system is installed. It covers all the windows on the lower level and all the doors."

"Then I'll feel perfectly safe when I have to be there all alone," she replied. He felt her gaze on him, warm and loving. "Although I feel safe whenever you're with me."

"But I can't be with you all the time." He tried to ignore the odd feeling of contentment that momentarily gripped him as he bathed in her obvious love for him. It wasn't real, this feeling of being...happy. It couldn't be real. He'd never expected to find happiness again.

It couldn't be real because he was a miserable bastard stuck in grief for his dead wife. It wasn't real because he'd been willing to do an unspeakable act to feed that grief. Finally, it wasn't real because everything he might feel for Julie or she might feel for him was based on a mountain of lies.

He consciously willed these thoughts away as he pulled into her driveway.

For the next twenty minutes he showed her how to work the alarm system.

"I set the code as 0615, but you can change it to whatever you want," he explained.

"Do those numbers mean something special to you?" she asked.

"No," he lied. "They're just random numbers that jumped into my head." But they weren't random numbers. It was actually the date his wife had been taken from him. It had been a beautiful June day that had ended his life as he'd known it.

He had consciously set those particular numbers to remind himself that he didn't belong there with Julie. He'd be reminded of that fact every time he entered Julie's house. This wasn't home and it never would be.

"Random numbers are good with me," she replied. She plopped down on the sofa. "I don't know if you've thought about what we're doing for dinner, but I was thinking maybe we'd just order in a pizza."

"That sounds good to me," he replied. "What I didn't get a chance to do today is check out the people on the list you gave me. I'd like to do some internet sleuthing this evening if you don't mind me using the laptop in the kitchen."

At least that task would take his mind off the sweet scent of her, off the crazy desire to somehow make all of this real.

"What kind of pizza do you like?" she asked.

"Pepperoni is my favorite, but I'll eat almost anything with pizza sauce and crust."

"My first choice is pepperoni, too." She appeared utterly pleased that they had this in common. "I'm going upstairs to change my clothes and order the pizza. Feel free to use the computer. It's not password protected. I'll be back down in a few minutes."

He breathed a sigh of relief as she headed up the stairs. He wasn't sure why he felt so vulnerable around her this evening. He'd been acutely aware of her from the moment he'd picked her up after work.

Maybe it was because he now knew that beneath her Peterson Pawn shop T-shirt her breasts were soft and welcoming, and he wanted to touch her again. He wanted to make love to her again, and that irritated him. The first time it had happened had been a terrible mistake. If it happened again, he deserved the firing squad.

He walked into the kitchen and pulled the list she had given him that morning out of his back pocket. He then sat at the built-in desk where a laptop awaited a touch of the power button.

There were seven names. Six men and one woman who worked at the pawn shop, along with the family members. If Julie believed something bad had happened in the shop, then all seven people were potential suspects in whatever Julie couldn't remember.

He was growing more and more ambivalent about her recovering her memories. He wanted her to remember what now had her in danger and yet he didn't want her to remember that she'd never known him before her accident. And that was wrong, so very wrong.

She needed to get her memories back so she would know their relationship wasn't real. She would hate him and throw him out of her life. It was possible she'd go to the police.

Maybe he deserved to be in jail. He'd had homicide in his heart on the night Brian McDowell had been murdered. Thinking about McDowell brought up thoughts of Debbie.

Before Nick could go completely down the rabbit hole, he typed in the first name on Julie's list.

Alexis Bellatore was twenty-seven years old and, according to her social media, she loved antiques, high heels and a man named Ben. She was a cute, slightly plump, woman with short, dark hair and big, dark eyes.

"If you sign into that account with my password, you'll be able to see all of her posts," Julie said from behind him.

He turned to see her in a light pink summer

dress that showcased her creamy shoulders and bare legs. A knot of simmering sparks leaped to life inside him.

She placed a hand on his shoulder and told him her password. "On this site, I'm friends with all the people on the list I gave you."

He typed in her password. "Thanks."

He hoped she would move. He wanted her to take her soft touch and sweet scent away from him. However, she remained.

In fact, she bent over and leaned closer. If he turned his head, she was close enough that he would be able to kiss her beautiful neck. And if that happened, there was no question in his mind she would encourage him to make love to her again.

He closed his eyes for a moment, filled with memories of how her silky skin had felt against his and how hot her mouth had tasted.

"Nick?"

Her laugh pulled him back from his lustful thoughts. He looked at the screen to realize he'd zoned out with his finger on the mouse and the screen now showed posts Alexis Bellatore had posted two years ago.

"Sorry, I zoned out for a minute," he said.

She laughed again, the sound as provocative as his previous thoughts. "I just wondered if you were some kind of an amazing speed reader and hadn't told me about that talent."

"Not hardly," he replied wryly. "I'm going to go through the last ten months of posts for each person and see if anything looks remotely suspicious."

"That's going to take a lot of time," she replied.

"I have plenty of time right now." In an effort to staunch the flames her nearness caused to burn inside him, he tried to conjure up thoughts of his wife.

What had Debbie smelled like? He frowned and stared at the computer screen, desperately trying to remember. He couldn't. All he could think about was the evocative floral scent of Julie.

Thankfully at that moment the doorbell rang. The pizza had arrived.

Minutes later they sat across from each other at the kitchen table.

"I'm not sure there's a better meal than warm pepperoni pizza and cold beer," she said and raised her napkin to wipe at a dab of errant sauce on her chin.

"Barbecue ribs and beer is a close second," he replied.

"I love all the foods that go with ribs…

potato salad, baked beans and maybe some garlic Texas toast. Hmm." She half closed her eyes with pleasure.

It was the same kind of look she'd worn when he'd made love to her. Dammit, what was wrong with him? Why did his thoughts keep going there? All he wanted was to solve her mystery, make sure she wasn't in any more danger and then he'd go his own way. He'd return to his life of grief and bitterness, of anger and misery.

They ate for a few minutes in silence. He was reaching for his third piece of the pie when she sat back in her chair and eyed him curiously.

"What?" he asked.

"I didn't know you liked ribs and pepperoni pizza, although I imagine I knew that before the accident. I was just wondering what else I've forgotten about you."

"You probably forgot that I squeeze the toothpaste tube in the middle," he replied lightly.

She grinned at him. "And I'm sure you remember that I do, too. What else?"

"There's that thing I do with my dirty socks."

"What thing?" she asked.

"Sometimes I forget to pick them up."

"Did I ever say anything about that?" Her eyes were a light denim blue that radiated pleasure.

"Oh, yeah. I believe more than once the word 'pig' popped into your vocabulary."

When her laughter stopped, he looked down at his slice of pizza and then returned his gaze to her. "I think you forgot that I've been married before."

Her eyes widened in shock. "I definitely forgot about that. How many times?"

"Just once." He picked up the slice of pizza from his plate.

"Did you get a divorce?"

He shook his head. Maybe, in talking about this, he'd remember the rage that had kept people at bay for the past three years. Maybe, if he went back to that horrendous day in his life, he'd remember why he wasn't good to anyone anymore.

"I'm a widower," he said. He dropped his pizza to the plate before him. "My wife Debbie was raped and murdered three years ago."

Julie's right hand moved to the base of her throat and her eyes were soft blue depths he wanted to jump into. Instead, once again, he looked down at his plate.

"Oh, Nick. I'm so sorry," she said. Her hand immediately covered one of his. "How did something so terrible happen? Or maybe you don't want to talk about it."

For the first time since it had happened, he realized he did want to talk about it. "Debbie was a real go-getter and very ambitious. She worked in high-end real estate and loved what she did. One evening she went to show a mansion to a man named Steven Winthrop."

He picked up his beer and took a long swallow, waiting for the rage that usually consumed him. When it didn't come, he continued. "He raped her in that big, empty house. He raped her and then he stabbed her." Julie gasped and he went on. "When she didn't check in with her office, one of her colleagues drove over to the house. She found her and called the police and me. I got there at the same time the police arrived."

Julie's hand tightened around his. "You don't have to tell me any more, Nick. I don't want you going back to that horrible moment in your life."

He closed his eyes, already in that moment, and he waited for the jagged, piercing anger and grief that always found him when he allowed himself to think of Debbie's death. It didn't come.

Instead a deep sadness touched him. A sadness absent of the killing anger. Was this acceptance? Had he finally reached the final stage of grief? He didn't know when or how it had happened.

"It's okay," he finally said. "I don't mind talking about it."

"What happened? Did this Steven Winthrop go to prison?"

Nick shook his head. "Initially he was brought in for questioning, but there wasn't enough evidence to charge him. He got away with murder."

"And you're sure he was guilty?" she asked softly.

"Absolutely. When I got to Debbie, she was one breath away from death. I asked her who did that to her and she said Winthrop."

"But wasn't that enough to get him charged and convicted?" she asked.

Nick sighed. "Unfortunately none of the police officers heard her, and Steven's wife alibied him by saying he never went to the showing, and there was no physical evidence tying him to the scene."

For a moment Nick remembered the angry

frustration that had coursed through him for months. "I begged the prosecutor to bring charges, to do something to get that man behind bars, but it didn't happen."

He squeezed Julie's hand and looked into her compassionate, caring, blue eyes. "It was a lifetime ago, Julie. I just needed to share it with you now so you know I'm carrying some baggage into this relationship."

He pulled his hand from hers, wondering what in the hell he was doing. He'd hoped that by talking about Debbie he'd distance himself from Julie, but now that he'd shared his pain with her, he felt closer to her than ever.

"I'm just sorry if you told me all this before that you had to repeat it all now," she said.

"And now we better finish up eating because I want to get back to the computer," he said. "I'm sorry I burdened you with all this."

"Nick, don't ever close off from me. I can handle your past. I can help you burden the pain."

This woman was killing him with her love. He got up from the table. "I'll keep that in mind," he replied, although that had been what he'd intended to do. He definitely felt the need to close off from her.

"I just want to get back to checking out

the people on the internet before another day passes. I'm hoping I'll find something that might bring your memories back to you."

He needed that to happen and damn the consequences. He needed to have her gain back her memories before he made the huge mistake of falling in love with her.

Chapter Nine

"I should just stay here with you tonight," Julie said as she came down the stairs. Her mother had called her earlier in the day to make a date for Julie to join Casey and her for a girls' night out.

"I won't be here tonight," Nick replied. "Remember I told you I was meeting with the other coaches this evening."

She walked over and plopped down next to him on the sofa. "I'd still just rather stay at home." She drew in the scent of him, the combination of minty soap and spicy cologne that always stirred her senses and made her feel safe.

She'd been disappointed last night that he hadn't slept with her. When she'd gone up to bed he'd still been on the computer and when she'd awakened this morning she noticed he hadn't joined her in the night. She'd thought they'd moved past any awkwardness where that issue was concerned.

"You told me you always enjoy spending time with your mom and sister," he said.

"Normally, I do, but I have a feeling tonight I'll be on the hot seat with Casey and Mom asking me far too many questions about you." She released a deep sigh, already anticipating the intense examination that would take place.

"Just go and have a little fun," he replied. "God knows you could use a little fun in your life right now."

"You're my fun."

He gazed at her soberly. "Enjoy your family while you have them, Julie. You never know when they'll be taken away from you."

Instantly she cursed herself for whining. Nick had not only lost his parents too soon, but he'd also lost his wife to a horrendous crime. "You're right," she replied.

She leaned forward and kissed him gently on the cheek. "And someday you and I will have children and we'll all be your family. Were you close to your parents?"

"Very close. As far as I'm concerned, I had the best parents in the world," he replied. "They encouraged and supported me in everything I did and, according to my grandmother, they spoiled me rotten."

A horn sounded from outside. She jumped up off the sofa. "Oh, I hate when Casey does that instead of coming to the front door. I'll be home by nine or so and then maybe you'll tell me some stories about your childhood."

He stood to walk her to the door. "I might be later than nine. I never know for sure how long these meetings are going to last. If you get home before me, just remember to set the alarm."

"Don't worry, I'll definitely remember the alarm." The horn honked again. "Geez, she makes me crazy. I'll see you later," she said. She walked out the front door to see an unfamiliar car in her driveway. Apparently, Casey had gotten a new car during the time Julie couldn't remember. Julie was surprised she could afford it, especially if what Joel had told her was true and their father had cut her off financially.

Casey was in the driver's seat and Julie's mother was in the passenger seat. Julie opened the back door and slid inside, the smell of new car and rich leather greeting her.

"About time," Casey said as she threw the car into Reverse. "I had to honk twice."

"You didn't have to honk at all," Julie replied drily. "You could have just texted me that you were here or actually walked up to the front door and knocked."

Casey grinned at her in the rearview mirror. "Honking is way more fun."

"I'm just glad to have both my girls with me tonight," Lynetta said. "I've been so crazed trying to organize the house to get it ready to show, I could use a little fun and a few drinks."

"The house ready to show?" Julie looked at the back of her mother's head in confusion.

Lynetta turned around in her seat to look at Julie. "Oh, honey, I guess you don't remember with your amnesia thing. Two months ago your daddy and I decided to downsize. We've already put down a deposit on a nice apartment at North Hills Village."

"But isn't that a retirement place?" Julie asked.

"It is. Of course, we all know your father will never retire. He'll probably drop dead in that pawn shop. But I'll definitely be retiring from cooking since all our meals will be prepared for us once we make the move." Lynetta turned back around.

Julie stared out the passenger window, her

head filled with thoughts of this surprising news. "Where are we going now?" she finally asked.

"Brewsters," Casey replied.

Brewsters was a lively bar that served strong drinks, great burgers and other bar food. The three women had often gone there for a night of hanging out together.

"Casey, when did you get this car?" she asked.

"I've had it for a little over a week now," she replied.

A little over a week? How could she afford such an expensive car if their father had cut her off and she scarcely worked at the shop? He must have caved to his baby girl, Julie thought, not that it was any of her business. Casey had always been the thoroughly spoiled child of the family.

"A mysterious boyfriend is helping her pay for it," Lynetta said, answering Julie's question. "I swear I don't know what's up with you two girls when it comes to the men in your life. Why does everything have to be such a deep, dark secret?"

"Maybe over dinner we can get Casey to spill some secrets about her boyfriend," Julie replied. It would be great if the spotlight was off her and Nick and on Casey instead. "Besides, I did eventually introduce you to Nick."

She didn't want to talk about Nick or their relationship. Despite the fact she'd apparently been dating him for a long time, it all felt so new and so very special right now.

Thankfully, Lynetta continued to talk about the retirement village and all the amenities it offered until they pulled into Brewsters' parking lot. "I'm ready for a nice, refreshing gin and tonic," she said as they all got out of the car.

"And I'm ordering some of their mozzarella sticks with a big Margarita. What about you, Julie?" Casey asked.

"I'm definitely ordering a burger and maybe some fried mushrooms on the side," she replied. "I'm not sure I want any alcohol tonight."

Although Julie couldn't remember the last time she'd been in the bar, stepping inside, she felt instantly at home. The air smelled of onions and burgers and all things fried. The old rock-and-roll music played loud enough to hear but not loud enough to impede conversation.

Lynetta slid into one of the black-leather

booths. Casey got in next to her and Julie sat across from them.

The menu was neatly printed on a large chalkboard behind the long, polished bar.

At least nothing on the menu had changed over the past ten months, Julie thought as the waitress approached their table. Minutes later they had all been served their drinks and had placed their food orders.

"So, how are things between you and Nick?" Casey asked.

"Couldn't be better," Julie replied. "Why don't you tell me more about this mysterious man you're dating?"

"Yes, I'd like to know more about him, too," Lynetta said. "Your father and I are worried about both of you with these secret boyfriends and fiancés popping up. You realize eventually you both will have a substantial inheritance and we don't want any man taking advantage of you."

"Ace isn't taking advantage of me, he's treating me right." Casey pointed to the purse on the booth seat next to her. "He bought this for me yesterday."

Julie recognized it as an expensive designer purse. "Pretty lavish. What does Ace do for a living?" she asked. Her sister had always had a penchant for bad boys.

"He's an entrepreneur," Casey replied.

"And what exactly does that mean?" Lynetta asked.

"It means he does a lot of stuff that I don't really understand, but it all makes him lots of money." Casey flipped a strand of her dark hair over her shoulder as if tossing Lynetta's concerns aside. "I don't understand his business stuff, but he's crazy about me and I'm crazy about him, and that's all that matters."

"How long have you been seeing him?" Julie took a sip of her soda and eyed her sister.

"About two months. It was love at first sight."

"Wasn't Granger love at first sight, too?" Julie asked drily. Granger was the last boyfriend she remembered Casey having. That "love at first sight" had lasted about two weeks.

"Granger is old, old news, and besides, that was just a silly crush," Casey replied. "Ace is the real deal," Casey said with certainty.

"And where did you meet this Ace?" Lynetta asked.

"At Freddy's," Casey replied.

Freddy's was a popular bar with a large

dance floor that featured local bands. It was also known as a singles pickup joint.

"Do you have a picture of him in your phone?" Julie asked.

"Nah, I haven't taken any of him yet," Casey replied.

"You? The selfie queen?" Lynetta looked at her youngest daughter in disbelief.

Casey grinned. "Oh, I have lots of pictures of me. I just don't have any of him yet."

"So, when do we all get to meet him?" Julie asked.

"In time," Casey replied. "I'm not quite ready to share him yet. Besides, you took months before you let us meet Nick."

Julie definitely understood her sister's desire to keep her man all to herself. That must have been the way she'd felt about Nick in the months before her accident.

Before anyone could say anything else, their meals arrived and the conversation turned to Lynetta and George's move.

"I'm surprised Dad agreed to sell the house," Julie said. "He's got so much stuff in it, I can't imagine how you're going to fit it all into a smaller place."

The family home was a huge old Victorian

with five bedrooms and enough "stuff" to fill several warehouses.

"We aren't. I told him he has to take his stuff and put it in the shop for sale or take it to the dump. I have to confess, he really didn't want to make this move, but I told him I was moving with or without him. We don't need all those bedrooms now that you kids are all grown and we definitely don't need a life-size statue of Elvis in our living room." Lynetta frowned. "I don't want second-hand junk in my personal space anymore. I want clean and new and efficient."

"You deserve the life you want," Julie replied with a warm smile at her mother. Lynetta had been a hardworking, hands-on kind of mom. She'd been strict but loving and had the patience of Job when it came to dealing with their father.

"Speaking of living the life you want, are you going to sell your house or is Nick selling his when you two get married?" Casey asked.

"To be honest, we haven't even discussed it," Julie replied. She hoped they'd decide to keep her place even though she had yet to see Nick's. In truth, she couldn't imagine Nick anywhere but in her home with her.

"I have to admit, I'm surprised you and Joel didn't wind up together."

Julie looked at her sister in surprise. "Me and Joel? Why on earth would you think there was anything romantic between us?"

"Before your amnesia, he was really into you," Casey replied.

"What do you mean? What are you talking about?" A faint roar sounded in Julie's ears. It was the roar of rich anger followed by a whimpering helplessness that she couldn't remember.

"About two months ago you talked to me and told me you thought Joel had a major crush on you. You really don't remember anything that happened before your accident?" Casey looked at her as if she were a bug under a microscope.

"Not much. A flash here and there, but so far I haven't been able to make much sense of them," Julie replied. "So, how did I feel about Joel having a crush on me?"

"A little creeped out," Casey replied. "At least, that's what you told me. I know he has lots of pictures of you up on his social media page, and that is definitely creepy."

Julie thought of the slightly overweight, easygoing Joel and a faint chill worked up her spine. Was it possible he was the one who had come through the pawn shop's back door on the night she'd forgotten her phone?

She had never been attracted to Joel on a romantic level, although she'd considered him a good friend and coworker. Had he somehow confronted her and professed his love for her that night and, when she wasn't interested in him, had he attacked her in some way?

She'd worked with him the day before and had sensed nothing off between them. He'd been his usual friendly and helpful self just like she remembered him from ten months ago.

But he'd also asked her a lot of questions about her amnesia during a lull in traffic at the shop. He'd asked what the doctors had told her about regaining her memories. Had she started to remember anything at all? Did she expect her memories to ever return?

Were they the normal questions that any person might ask of somebody suffering from amnesia? Or were they the questions of an attacker assuring himself that he was still safe?

NICK LEFT JULIE'S place at just after seven, grateful that cloud cover would make the darkness of night arrive early. Since the time

Julie had left the house, Nick had been consumed with thoughts of murder. And, thank God, on this night in particular, she'd had plans with her mother and sister, because he'd lied to her once again. He wasn't meeting with his fellow coaches. He was meeting with the men who'd planned not only Brian's murder, but the murders of five other people, as well.

The minute Julie had left the house he'd used the internet to check every local news source he could to see if there were any updates on the McDowell murder. He'd found nothing. He hated to be out of the loop on a matter that could touch his life in such a negative way.

He'd spent the rest of the evening pacing, contemplating what might come tonight when he met the others. The six of them had originally gotten to know each other at the Northland Survivor group meetings. However, since that time, four of the men had stopped going to the meetings. They didn't want a place where they were all connected should the police get close to them.

After the meeting, after complete darkness fell, they would all meet at the Oak Ridge Park. The space had once been a popular place for people to picnic and play baseball, but over the years better parks had been built. Now the trees and bushes, the grass and weeds, had encroached in an attempt to take back what had once been theirs.

The Northland Survivor meeting took place in the basement of a Methodist church, although it wasn't church sponsored.

At six fifty that evening, he pulled into the parking lot and steeled himself for sitting through the meeting. All he really wanted to do was to talk to the others about the fact that he had not been the one who had killed Brian McDowell. Somebody had committed that murder mere minutes before Nick had arrived.

As always, the meeting room smelled of strong, fresh coffee and deep, abiding grief. Janet McCall, the founder of the group, greeted him as he walked in.

Janet had been married for fifteen years when her husband had been brutally murdered as he'd left a downtown restaurant after a business meeting. When his body had been found, his wallet was empty and his cell phone was gone. He'd been killed for fifteen bucks and a phone.

According to Janet, her grief had nearly driven her to suicide.

Instead of taking a complete grief-stricken head-dive, she had started this group for people to talk and hopefully heal.

"How have you been, Nick?" Her brown eyes studied his features carefully.

"Not too bad," he replied.

"I can see a new lightness about you." She smiled at him warmly. "I'm glad. Now, get yourself a cup of coffee and don't forget to try one of my lemon bars."

"Will do," he replied. As he walked over to the refreshment table, he thought about what Janet had said about a new lightness in him. And that lightness had a name—Julie.

She had given him something indefinable, something that had brought him back from the brink of despair. With her, he'd found his laughter again. He was looking forward rather than backward. He didn't know what his future might hold, but for the first time since Debbie's murder, he actually believed he had a future.

If he wasn't arrested for a murder he hadn't committed.

He carried his coffee to sit in one of the folding chairs that formed a large circle. He nodded at several familiar people, including Troy Anderson. Three years ago, Troy's eight-year-old daughter had been kidnapped and killed. Troy was one of the six men who had come together in their need-for-vengeance pact.

Within minutes, people began to fill the seats. This group wasn't just about the collateral damage left behind by murder. It was also for anyone who had lost somebody in their life and was dealing with debilitating grief.

By the time Janet began to facilitate the meeting, there was only one unfamiliar face in the group. A heavyset woman with bleached-blond hair and heavy blue eyeliner sat next to Janet.

"Before we get started this evening, I'd like to introduce Jacqueline Kelly, who is with us for the first time." Janet placed a hand on the woman's thick shoulder. "Jacqueline, can you tell us what brought you here tonight?"

Huge tears welled up in her eyes as she looked around. "I'm here because my boyfriend was murdered and I don't know what I'm going to do without him." A huge sob choked out of her. "He helped take care of me and my kids, and he was murdered right in his own house. Somebody came in and slit Brian's throat." She began to weep in earnest.

Nick froze. His heart stopped and then beat so fast a whoosh of blood filled his head and momentarily deafened him. There was no question that she was talking about the man Nick had seen dead behind a shattered sliding-glass door. A man Nick had been prepared to murder.

As his hearing returned, he listened to Jacqueline's keening grief. God, he knew that grief so intimately. Yet, in the midst of his rage, he'd never considered that the people they'd intended to kill might have girlfriends or wives or daughters and sons. That they could have other family members and best friends who would deeply mourn their deaths.

The pact he'd made with the other men now felt more than a little bit evil. No matter who they murdered, it wouldn't bring Debbie or any of their loved ones back. He wasn't sure if he'd actually been able to pull the trigger to kill Brian McDowell or not. All he was certain of was his huge need to speak with the other men and maybe try to call a halt to their collective madness.

The rest of the meeting was a study in torture for Nick. He tried not to look at Jacqueline and he also kept his gaze averted from Troy.

During the fifteen-minute break, he got another cup of coffee and one of Janet's lemon bars, and then returned to his seat. The program for tonight was being led by a psychologist who would speak about the power of forgiveness.

Nick only half listened to the plump professional, who had a dreadful, monotonic delivery and stood perfectly still as he spoke. Instead, Nick watched the big round clock on the wall, inching toward the time to end the meeting.

It was just after nine when the meeting adjourned.

Once again Nick was grateful for the cloud cover that made for an early nightfall. Talk of murder deserved to be in the darkness.

He clenched the steering wheel tight as he drove to the park, a large ball of tension rolling around in the pit of his stomach.

He was certain one of the other men had killed McDowell. Was it possible that somehow wires had gotten crossed? Adam Kincaid had taken the lead in the plan that had been hatched. He'd made sure the left hand didn't know what the right hand was doing. Had he somehow made a mistake?

It didn't matter now. Brian McDowell was dead. What did matter was that Nick intended to try to talk the other men into halting this madness...this lust for vengeance they had all fallen victim to.

Was justice really theirs to deliver? Who did they think they were to be the arbiters of death? He had to believe that somehow karma took care of things. He needed to believe that the guilty eventually paid a price, whether in this life or the next. But what he had planned with the five other men had been wrong.

Seeing Jacqueline had put a new spin on things for him. Or was it Julie's presence in his life that had calmed the beast inside him? He didn't know the answer, but he felt a huge shift had occurred inside him.

He pulled into the parking lot of the abandoned park and drove straight ahead, off the broken asphalt and across the old ball field toward a stand of trees.

He was the first one to arrive. He parked and then grabbed a flashlight from his glove compartment. He got out of the car and headed deeper into the woods.

Once he reached the designated meeting

place, he eased down onto a fallen tree trunk to wait. A faint breeze whispered through the treetops and all around him the night insects clicked and whirred. Cicadas played their noisy rhythm as if telling him he didn't belong there.

And he didn't. He was ready to close this chapter of his life. Whatever his future might hold, he didn't want to carry the rage, the all-consuming grief and that bloodlust inside him anymore.

"Hey." Troy Anderson's deep voice pulled Nick out of his thoughts. "Intense meeting for you, huh. You okay?"

"Yeah, I'm better than I've been in years," Nick replied. There was no point in telling Troy about McDowell and Nick's change of heart before the other men arrived. He would just have to repeat himself.

"I guess tonight just proves it's a small world. Who would have thought McDowell's girlfriend would show up at the same meeting as you," Troy said.

"Yeah, who would have thought," Nick replied.

Before any further discussion could occur, Matt Tanner and Clay Rogers arrived.

Matt immediately walked over to Nick

and patted him on the shoulder. "Thank you, man," he said, and Nick knew he was congratulating him on killing the person who had beaten Matt's mother to death and had gotten away with the crime. "I'm so glad that bastard is dead."

"Don't thank me yet," Nick replied.

Matt looked at him curiously, but at that moment Adam Kincaid and Jake Lamont stepped into the small clearing.

The unholy six men were together again.

Nick became aware that the woods had quieted. The insects had stopped clicking and the cicadas had stopped singing as if in disapproval of this covert meeting.

"We need to make this fast," Adam said. "You know we're all at risk when we're together."

"I didn't kill Brian McDowell," Nick said without preamble.

"What are you talking about?" Adam turned on a flashlight and directed it at Nick's face. "I sent you everything to kill him. You were the one I assigned to kill him, and I saw in the paper the report of his murder."

"Somebody got to him before me." Nick squinted against the brightness of Adam's flashlight and told the men about the night he had gone to kill McDowell. "If one of you didn't jump the gun, then somebody else is in on the game."

"Nobody else better be in on the game," Adam said. "That puts us all at risk."

All the other men vehemently denied having told anyone of the plan. "I want out," Nick said. "I think all of us should just forget this whole idea and get on with our lives."

"No way," Troy said, anger lacing his deep voice. "You're just saying that because you saw Jacqueline cry at the meeting. Just remember, if she'd had anything he'd wanted, he would have killed her to get it. He beat Matt's mother to death. We did her a favor by getting him out of her life. Besides, I want the man who killed my daughter dead. I want him dead so he can't prey on any other little girls."

"And I can't tell you how good it feels to know Brian McDowell will never kill a vulnerable old woman again," Matt said, his voice also rich with emotion. "This is a good plan. We're taking out killers who we all know would probably re-offend."

"Doesn't it bother you all that somebody got to Brian on the exact night, at the exact time, I was supposed to act?" Nick asked as he looked from man to man.

"McDowell was a creep. Creeps make enemies. It was probably just a weird coincidence that somebody got to him right before you did," Jake stated.

"I don't think so," Nick replied. "I don't know which one of you is responsible, but one of you killed him."

When none of the others spoke, Nick released a deep sigh. "I've said what I came here to say. I don't want this to go forward. I don't want to be a part of it and I definitely don't want one of you to kill Steven Winthrop. Nobody should have his blood on their hands. Let karma take care of him. In any case, he'll burn in hell for what he did." He'd said what he needed to say and there was nothing more that he could do.

"We're all in this together," Adam said sharply. "Anyone else have doubts about what we're doing?" He looked at each of the other men. "Anyone else want out?"

"We're all still in," Matt said firmly.

"Then I suggest we get out of here," Adam replied. "Wait for your instructions and keep your mouths shut."

"I'm out of here for good," Nick said. "My

assignment is finished and there's no reason for me to meet here again. Don't worry, I will take this secret to the grave with me, but I'm in a place where all I want to do now is build my future."

Minutes later Nick was in his car and headed toward home. No, he corrected himself. He was headed toward Julie's place. It would never be his home.

He was ready to build a future, but how could Julie be a part of it? How long could he continue to live a lie? The longer they were together, the more difficult it would be when the truth finally came out.

A headache began to pound at his temples and a wave of soul-sickness, of utter exhaustion, overtook him. He had no idea who had killed Brian McDowell, but suspected one of the others was responsible. He'd been stark raving mad when he'd agreed to the vigilante plot in the first place.

That time in his life would always haunt him. The men who continued on the path of seeking justice would haunt him, as well. Even if they found the justice they sought, they would realize it was an empty reward.

He released a deep sigh and tried to empty his brain.

He was in love with Julie.

The sudden realization momentarily stole the breath from his lungs. Someway, since the night of the accident, Julie had become far more than a convenient alibi. She'd become the woman he wanted to spend the rest of his life with.

He'd be a fool to believe there was any hope for a future with her. He now had to figure out how to gain some emotional distance from her. He had to stop loving her.

More importantly, he had to make her stop loving him.

Chapter Ten

The minute Julie got home from dinner she sat at her desk and pulled up Joel's social media page. Looking in his picture section, she was surprised by all the photos she saw of herself.

Yet, as she looked at them carefully, memories began to blossom in her mind. She remembered three months ago when a customer had come in with a hat shaped like a snarling, long-toothed vampire. Her father had loved it and bought it. Julie had put it on, made a face, and Joel had taken a picture of her.

They had taken selfies together. He'd snapped a picture of her while she was dusting the jewelry display counter and another when she'd had her first bite of sushi for lunch.

Excitement and confusion filled her at the same time. She remembered in detail when each and every photograph had been taken, and that excited her. What confused her was why Casey would have thought the pictures were somehow creepy in any way.

They were just the kind of pictures coworkers...friends took of each other. They were ordinary photos. It wasn't like he had secretly taken pictures of her grocery shopping or getting out of her car in her driveway, as if he were stalking her.

But apparently she'd told Casey she'd thought Joel had a crush on her. She'd told her sister she'd been creeped out by it, and that's what had her confused.

She'd worked with Joel several days since her accident and hadn't gotten any strange vibes off him. Had he done something terrible to her that she just couldn't remember?

She started as she heard the front door open. The alarm system began its countdown to full siren, but halted when the code was punched in. Nick was home.

She jumped out of the chair, eager to see him, to find out how his meeting had gone and to talk to him about what Casey had said about Joel.

He walked into the living room at the same time she did. His shoulders cast forward slightly and he looked totally drained of energy.

"Nick, are you all right?" She grabbed him by the hand and led him to the sofa. "You look exhausted. Did something happen at your meeting?"

He pulled his hand from hers and sat back. "No, everything went fine. I'm just beyond exhausted tonight. How did your dinner go?"

"The same as they always go. It was fine." She studied his features. The lines of his face that she'd always found attractive were now deeper and his eyes were without their usual brightness. "Nick, go on to bed. You look absolutely sick with exhaustion."

"I think I'll do that." He pulled himself to his feet.

"You can sleep as late as you want in the morning," she said as she also rose from the sofa. "For the next few days, I'm working the evening shift."

He nodded, as if just too tired to speak. With a wave of his hand, he headed toward the stairs.

She watched him go, wishing he'd join her in her bed, but knowing he'd go to the guest room.

She'd wanted to talk to him about Joel.

She'd wanted to tell him about Casey's new boyfriend and that her parents were moving, and she'd wanted to hear all about his meeting. But all that could wait until morning.

She returned to the kitchen where she turned off the computer.

It was late enough she was ready for a good night's sleep, as well. She climbed the stairs, a touch of worry and guilt rising inside her.

He'd said his meeting had gone fine, but she wasn't sure she believed it. What if the other coaches had given him a bad time about being so absent? Had he not told her that football practices had already begun and he wasn't attending them because he was too busy babysitting her?

The last thing she wanted to do was to cause him trouble where he worked. How much was she really interfering in his life? Or maybe she was just imagining things. Maybe he was simply a tired man and everything would be fine in the morning.

However, the next morning he was unusually quiet and withdrawn as they sat together at the table having coffee.

"Is something wrong, Nick? Have I done something wrong?"

"Not at all. Why do you ask?" His eyes were dark, guarded, as he gazed at her.

"You just seem rather distant," she replied.

"I've got a lot of things on my mind." He raised his cup to his lips and averted his gaze from hers.

"Is there anything I can help with?" She hated seeing him this way, without the sparkle in his eyes and the beautiful smile on his lips.

"No. I've just got some things I need to work through in my head. So, tell me about your dinner last night."

"We went to Brewsters," she began.

"I love their food. Several of us sometimes go in there to get a tenderloin sandwich after games."

"I've never tried their tenderloin. I'm all about their fried mushrooms," she replied, pleased to see him start to relax as his eyes began to sparkle.

"Nothing better than good, fried bar food. I'm glad you're a woman who doesn't eat rabbit food for every meal."

She laughed. "That's so not me. Sure, I watch my weight, but I also indulge my love of junk food whenever I can."

"Were there any surprises last night? Any flashes of memory?"

She shook her head. "The biggest surprise is that I didn't remember that my parents are in the process of moving into a senior living place. I didn't have any flashes of memory until I got back here."

He raised a brow. "What happened when you got back here?"

She explained to him what Casey had told her about Joel. "I remembered when all the pictures were taken as I looked at them. He does have a lot of pictures of me on his social media, but remembering when they were taken, they don't seem odd at all to me."

"And you didn't get any strange feelings about Joel?"

"None. But Casey said before the accident I was creeped out about him. I've worked with him a couple of times since the accident and I haven't felt creeped out at all." An edge of frustration leaped into her voice. "Dammit, I need my memories back right now."

"I know you're anxious to get them back." He paused to take a drink of his coffee. "I didn't get to Joel when I was checking social media for all the people who worked at the shop. He was one of the last names you wrote down." He drained his coffee cup and stood. "Let me check him out right now." He moved from the table to the hard-backed chair in front of the desk.

She got up and walked over to stand just behind him, enjoying the freshly showered scent of him that stirred a sweet, hot desire inside her. As he waited for the computer to boot up, she moved even closer to him and placed her hands on his shoulders.

She loved the play of his muscles beneath his T-shirt. She remembered how his warm, bare skin had felt against her when they'd made love.

She hungered to repeat the experience. Even though she didn't have her memories of him before, at least they were building new memories together every day.

He pulled up Joel's pages and leaned forward, displacing her hands from him. "You specifically remember when these were all taken?" he asked.

"Each and every one," she replied. "And I didn't feel anything odd or creepy when we took them. We were just goofing around at work."

He turned around in the chair and she

stepped back from him. "And yet you told your sister he was creeping you out."

"That's what Casey told me."

They moved back to the kitchen table. "I worked with him and didn't feel a bit uncomfortable," she repeated, struggling to make sense of it all.

"When do you work with him again?"

"I think maybe tomorrow night," she replied. "But I think my dad is on the schedule that night, too."

Nick held her gaze intently. "Have you told your family about everything that's going on?"

"No. I haven't mentioned anything about the phone call or the doll. I haven't told them that somebody is after me for something I'm not supposed to tell."

"Why haven't you told them?"

She frowned thoughtfully. She knew the answer and she was slightly ashamed to say it out loud. "Right now the only person I completely trust in the whole wide world is you."

"Then you think one of your family members is responsible?" He looked at her with a touch of surprise.

"I don't know," she replied, the frustration back in her voice. "I certainly don't want to believe that, but right now I don't feel comfortable talking to any of them about this. There's a little voice in the back of my head that keeps whispering I should keep all this a secret where they are concerned."

"You need to remember, Julie."

"I know, but I feel like the harder I try, the less likely it is to happen." Anxiety tightened her chest. Her missing memories not only had her at risk, but she also thought some of the distance she felt from Nick was because of those missing memories.

"Nick, my lack of memories shouldn't play a role in our relationship," she said softly. "Even if I don't remember being in love with you, I'm falling in love with you all over again." She felt the warmth that leaped into her cheeks at this confession.

He scooted his chair away from the table and stood. "But it does make a difference to me. Every time I touch you, I feel like I'm taking advantage of you because you can't remember me."

"I love it when you touch me. Nick, the last thing you're doing is taking advantage of me. If anything, I'm taking advantage of you by wanting you here with me all the time. The last thing I want to do is interfere with your work."

"Speaking of work, I do have some phone calls and other business to attend to this morning. If you don't mind, I'll just head on up to my bedroom to get to it." He looked at some point just over the top of her head. "Just let me know if you need anything."

She watched him go, her heart thudding a dull rhythm. Was he tired of her? Tired of the drama that filled her life right now? She couldn't blame him if he was. He'd been a prisoner to her drama, trapped with her because somebody was after her and she couldn't remember why. Dammit, she was tired of it all.

She didn't remember loving him, but she had to do something to remind him of loving her. She just wasn't sure what to do to change the dynamics between them right now.

Somehow they had gotten all messed up since the night they had made love. She desperately needed to remember everything that remained in the shadows of her mind. She felt as if everything she held dear was slipping away from her.

Three days later nothing had changed. Nick continued to be distant and Julie continued to fear that the man of her dreams was about to walk out of her life.

They were a subdued pair as Nick drove her to work at four o'clock. The past three days had been difficult ones. Between meals, he'd kept himself holed up in his bedroom. During meals, their conversations were slightly strained.

She released a deep sigh as he pulled up at the pawn shop's back door. "I'll be back here at nine thirty to pick you up," he said, his gaze focused on the steering wheel.

She reached out and curled her fingers around his upper arm. "Nick," she said. His green eyes finally looked at her. "I don't know what's going on between us right now, but I don't like it. You're withdrawing from me and I don't know what to do about it. I miss you. I miss us."

His eyes darkened in hue. He reached out and dragged a finger gently down her cheek. "I'm going through some things right now, Julie." He pulled his finger back as if her skin had burned him. "I just need a little space."

"Is it anything I can help with? I mean, whatever is happening, we're in this together, right?" She fought the impulse to tighten her fingers on him, the desire to keep him close to her forever.

He shook his head. "This is something I need to work through myself."

What issue could he have that he was working on? She wanted to ask him if they were in trouble. If his feelings for her had changed. But she was afraid of the answer so she didn't ask. "Okay, then… I'll see you later," she said and got out of his car.

As she opened the door to the pawn shop she wasn't sure what she feared most: the person who had left the doll for her or the possibility that Nick might leave her.

She'd never been a needy person before. But her life felt so wildly out of control right now and Nick was the only thing substantial she had to hang on to.

She was grateful that she was working with Max, even though he was irritated that he was taking over Casey's shift. Apparently, Casey had the flu. At least, that's what she'd told Max when she'd called him to tell him she couldn't work tonight.

Julie was glad to work with her older brother, who was superefficient and quick in dealing with customers. Casey usually flirted with all the men who came in and took forever to do a fairly simple pawn or sale. Julie also spent half her time working with Casey trying to get her out of the office where she'd sit and paint her fingernails or talk on her cell phone.

Still, it was a fairly difficult and busy night. Whenever the end of the month approached, more people came in to pawn items, desperate for a little money to get them by until their disability or pay check came in after the first of the month.

It was getting toward the end of the night when Ed Graham walked in. Julie stifled a groan. Ed was a frequent customer and usually threw a tizzy fit when they didn't offer him what he believed his "treasures" were worth. It was funny that she remembered him but couldn't remember the really important things in her life.

Max was busy ringing up a woman who was buying dozens of DVDs and Julie steeled herself as Ed stalked up to the counter.

"Ed." She greeted him with a pleasant smile that he didn't return.

"You've got to do me right this time," he said. "You've screwed me over and over again, but I need three hundred bucks until the third of the month." He dug into his pocket and withdrew a pocket watch. "This belonged to my daddy and his daddy before him." For a moment he held it tightly in his meaty fist and then laid it down on the countertop.

Julie grabbed a jeweler's loop and took a closer look at it. There was nothing special about the watch. It wasn't even fourteen karat gold.

"Ed, I can't give you anywhere close to three hundred dollars for this," she said.

"Dammit, Julie. It's an antique. It's got to be worth that." His broad face began to flush with anger and his nostrils flared. "So, how much can you give me?"

"No more than fifty," Julie replied.

"Fifty?" The word exploded out of him like a gunshot. "You've got to be out of your freaking mind." He grabbed the watch and shoved it back in his pants' pocket. "I knew you'd try to screw me again. You all are nothing but a pack of shysters. This will be the last time I'll ever come in here to do business."

As he stormed out the door, Max looked over at Julie and grinned. "He'll be back. He always comes back."

Julie knew Max was right. Ed Graham was one of their regulars and, if he stayed true to form, he'd be back tomorrow or the day after and take whatever they were willing to give him for the pocket watch.

It was just after nine when she and Max found themselves alone in the shop. "Since I wasn't even on the schedule to work tonight, can you close up so I can go ahead and get out of here?" he asked.

"No problem," she replied. Nick would arrive at nine thirty to pick her up and she certainly didn't anticipate a rush of customers at this time of night. It was rare that anyone came in after nine in the evening.

Minutes later Max was gone and Julie was by herself in the shop. And it didn't take her long to feel a little creeped out. She checked the clock. Ten after nine. To hell with it, she was closing up shop now.

Out of one of the cash registers' drawers, she grabbed the key she needed to lock up and then headed for the front door. She'd just locked the door when the lights went out.

She froze. What now? Did a fuse blow? It happened rarely, but it did happen. The only illumination now was from a nearby streetlight and that barely seeped into the shop.

There was a rush of air as a big shadow appeared out of the darkness. The shadow slammed into her. Her breath expelled out of her as she flew backward and to the floor.

The back of her head banged against the wood and a moan escaped her.

Still, she scrabbled backward using her feet and elbows, her brain frozen with fear. Not a shadow…a person. And there was no question that he intended to hurt her.

She gasped for breath and finally released a scream as he grabbed her by the ankle and began to pull her toward him.

His grip was strong, so damned strong. Kicking and twisting, in the back of her mind she knew this wasn't a robbery attempt. In the faint light she saw him: a well-built man clad all in black and wearing a ski mask.

If he wanted to rob the store, he could have just waited fifteen minutes for her to leave. In horror she recognized he was after her. He'd been hiding someplace in the store and had waited to attack until she was all alone.

"What do you want?" she screamed as she fought to get away from him.

"I want to make sure you never tell what you know," he roared. He threw himself on top of her and wrapped his gloved hands around her throat.

Her scream was a mere gurgle as he tightened his hold on her. She tried to gasp for air, but there was none. He growled like a wild animal as he kept her pinned to the floor, his hands squeezing…squeezing…squeezing the very life out of her.

Her instinct was to grab his hands to try to pull them away from her throat as she weakened with every second. Instead she poked at his eyes in desperation as darkness began to seep around the edges of her consciousness.

One of her jabs finally hit its mark. He roared in pain and released his hold. She rolled away from him, gasping for air, and then staggered to her feet and ran.

"You bitch," he yelled.

The darkness was her friend now. She knew the inside of the pawn shop like the back of her hand. She moved silently among the shelves, working her way toward the office where she could either lock herself inside or escape out the back door.

Nick, where are you? How much time was left before he arrived? She stifled a scream as the man snarled again. He was like a panther hunting prey. A crash sounded, followed by another curse. Another crash…this one closer.

Suddenly he was there. She saw only the big, dark bulk of him, standing between her and the back door. She veered to the left and headed toward the second room.

She entered the room, her mind frantically trying to think of a hiding place. The man was definitely too big and strong for her to try to fight. The only way she would survive this night was if she hid until Nick arrived.

Nick. Her heart cried his name. Wasn't it time for him to be there? God, it felt like a lifetime had passed since the lights in the shop had gone off.

Would the man find her behind the genie? She definitely didn't want to run into the bathroom. Even though it had a lock, she knew the man could get through the flimsy hollow wood door and then she'd be at a dead end with no escape possible.

She suddenly remembered the large penguin had a hidey-hole in its belly and that's where she went. She crouched down and slapped a hand over her mouth to silence the screams that begged to be released. Her heart beat so fast she felt dizzy.

"Julie."

The voice whispered so close by she imagined she could feel his fetid breath on her neck. Her heart stopped beating as she realized despite her frantic thinking she'd put herself in a space with no exit.

If he found her, she'd have nowhere to run.

Chapter Eleven

Nick parked outside the pawn shop's back door and got out of his car. He paused and drew a deep breath. He was exhausted. Trying to maintain emotional and physical distance from Julie was much more difficult than he'd imagined.

After Debbie died, he never thought he'd fall in love again, but now he couldn't figure out how to stop loving Julie. Was this his karma for even thinking about taking somebody else's life? That he would fall in love and see a future filled with happiness for himself but it would not be his to obtain?

He looked up at the moon, a thousand regrets sweeping through him. He felt as if he were a locomotive barreling down the tracks into a brick wall.

He released a deep sigh. The last thing he wanted to do was to stand outside in the dark and think of all the crazy twists and turns his life had taken since he'd made the pact with five other grieving men.

He opened the shop's back door and blinked at the darkness that greeted him. Every muscle tensed. What in the hell was going on?

"Julie?"

"Nick!" Fear laced her voice, which was oddly muffled and came from someplace to his right.

He took several steps in that direction and gasped as somebody shoved him from behind. He turned in time to see a man disappear out the back door.

"Hey!" Nick yelled after him at the same time his heart did a nosedive. Julie! What had the man done to her? Was she hurt someplace in the dark?

"Julie, where are you? Are you okay?" Dammit, without the lights he would have a hard time finding her.

"I'm here."

"Keep talking, honey, and I'll find you."

"Max left early and…and…the man must have hidden in the shop."

Her voice came from his right again and even though he wanted to run to her, he walked carefully through the darkness.

"He…he attacked me when I locked the front door." Her voice was louder now. "Is he gone?"

"He's gone. Honey, it's safe for you to come out now."

"Okay, I'm coming out." He heard her words right before she flew out of the darkness and into his arms.

"Thank God," she cried, her entire body trembling against him.

"What happened? Did he hurt you?" he asked.

She shook her head, unable to speak around her deep sobs.

"Come on, let's go outside." He wasn't comfortable standing in the dark shop. He didn't know where the man had gone when he'd run out of the shop. Or if he'd come back.

She clung to him as he moved them out of the shop and next to his car. He gazed around in all directions, tensing for any danger that might come out of the night. But he saw nobody.

Finally Julie's sobs eased enough that she could talk.

"He wanted to kill me," she said. She raised her head to look at him and in the depths of her eyes he saw her terror. "He…he said he'd make sure I never told what I know." A burst of hysterical laughter escaped her. "It must be one hell of a secret I've got in my stupid mind."

"We need to call the police." Nick grabbed his cell phone out of his pocket.

"And call my father," she said. "He needs to know what's going on."

Julie sat in the safety of his car while he made the calls and then he joined her there to wait for the others to arrive. He started the engine so the air conditioner would cool them down.

"He must have been hiding inside," she said. Her voice trembled and her face was shockingly pale in the light from the dash. "He waited until Max left. I locked the front door and the lights suddenly went out and then he attacked me." One of her hands rose to her throat. "He tried to strangle me but I managed to poke him in the eye and get away. I hide in that big penguin."

"I'm so sorry, Julie." He reached out and grabbed her hand. "I'm sorry you had to go through that." It was obvious now that they had underestimated the enemy. The danger was real. It had come out of nowhere and had almost been deadly.

He squeezed her hand. "Thank God you got away." The back of his throat threatened to close up as he thought of what might have happened tonight.

Before he could say anything else, a police car pulled into the parking lot. The lights swirled blue and red colors that splashed across the back of the building.

They both got out of the car to greet the two officers who had responded to his call.

Nick placed his arm around Julie's shoulder as she explained what had happened.

The officers asked them both questions about the description of the person who had attacked her, but neither of them could say anything that helped. Nick hadn't even known the man wore a ski mask until Julie told the officers. Julie also told them about the phone call and the doll that had been left hanging in the doorway on her deck.

By that time George arrived. He jumped out of his car, a grim expression on his face. "What in the hell happened here?"

Julie briefly filled her father in on what had occurred in the shop.

However, the one thing she didn't tell George was about the man making it clear that he intended to kill her because of a secret she possessed.

With the aid of the officers' flashlights, George discovered the breaker in the office had been flipped, causing the electricity to shut off.

With the lights back on again, they all went inside where George cursed at the loss of a large decorative vase that lay shattered on the floor and a television that had been knocked over and cracked.

"There had to be more than one person involved," Julie said. Her face was still void of her natural color. "Somebody had to be in the office to flip the breaker while the other person attacked me."

Nick's blood chilled. He hadn't considered that before. Having one person threatening her by phone and by leaving a horrible doll on her deck was one thing. Knowing there was more than one person involved was far more ominous.

He and Julie stayed in the office while Officer Jason Killion and Officer Mark Bradford checked out the place with George.

Nick and Julie waited in silence. The situation didn't warrant small talk and Julie appeared too shell-shocked to want any conversation.

She looked small and frail sitting in the chair in front of the desk. He hated it. He never wanted to see her as frightened as she was for the rest of her life.

Finally, George and the two officers joined Nick and Julie in the office. "There isn't much we can do at this point," Officer Killion said. "You told us he wore gloves, so there's no point in trying to fingerprint anything. And without any kind of description of the perp, we wouldn't know where to begin to find him."

"Call us if anything else occurs to you or if you remember something that would help us get the perpetrators," Officer Bradford said to Julie.

"Trust me, you'll be the first people I call," Julie replied.

Within minutes the officers were gone. "From now on, you aren't left alone in the store," George said to Julie.

"From now on, Julie is on vacation," Nick replied.

Julie gazed at him gratefully and George frowned in obvious irritation.

"Julie knows this place can't function without her, especially on such short notice," he said. "Tell him, girly. Tell him I need you here."

"I think I need some time off," Julie said softly. She didn't look at her father. "Dad, somebody tried to kill me tonight. I'm sorry, but until we figure out what's going on, I don't want to come in to work."

Nick watched as George's expression softened. "Okay, I'll figure things out here," he said. "Take all the time you need, honey."

"I'm taking her home right now," Nick said, knowing what she needed now more than anything was the sense of safety she would find at home behind locked doors.

George nodded. "Call me and let me know how you're doing," he said to Julie. "You know this was probably some sort of robbery attempt. Probably some druggie looking for a quick score of things he could fence."

"You need to install a camera in the second room so we can see from the office if anyone is in there at closing time," Julie replied.

"I'll get it done this week," George replied.

Minutes later Nick and Julie were headed home. "Thank you for telling my dad I was taking a bit of a vacation," she said. "I don't think I could face going back in there tomorrow night. I've never been so afraid in my entire life."

"I never want to see you that afraid again," Nick replied. Even thinking about what she'd experienced caused his heart to leap into his throat.

"I just wish I knew what was going on." She released a deep, tremulous sigh. "Maybe it's time I contact the doctor and get a referral to somebody who can help me retrieve my missing memories. Maybe I need to see a hypnotist and see if he or she can help me."

"I want you to do whatever it takes to get well." It was true. Nick wanted her to regain her memories because that might be the only thing that saved her from the people who wanted her dead.

It would be the death of his relationship with her but, more than anything, he wanted her safe. Eventually she'd forget about the man who had lied to her and she'd find a good man who would fulfill all her dreams.

A wave of dark depression descended upon him. It was the same feeling he'd had in the days and weeks after Debbie's murder before the rage had overtaken him.

He knew with certainty the self-destructive fury he'd felt at that time was gone forever, and yet it had been that anger that had brought Julie to him.

If he hadn't gone to Brian McDowell's house to kill him, then he wouldn't have been on the street when Julie had wrecked her car. He wouldn't be with her now, already mourning the loss of her in his life.

"I need to take a shower," she said the minute they got inside. "I need to wash off the feel...the smell of him that I have on my skin."

"Is there anything I can do?" he asked. God, he wanted to do something—anything—to help her wipe away the memory of her attacker.

Her gaze held his and in the depths of her eyes he saw the shadowed darkness of trauma. "Just be here for me," she said.

"Julie, I'm here for you and only you," he replied.

She held his gaze for another long moment and then nodded and walked slowly up the stairs.

He watched her until she disappeared from sight. *Just be here for me.* Her words haunted him as he sank down on the sofa. Tonight had scared the hell out of him. While he'd been standing outside and ruminating about his life, Julie had been inside fighting for her very life.

What if he'd waited three minutes longer before entering the back door? What if he'd waited five more minutes? The odds were good the man would have eventually found Julie's hiding place. What if she hadn't been able to physically fight him off in the first place?

He'd lost love once to a violent, unspeakable act by another person. The last thing he wanted to do was to lose Julie to the same kind of death or any other kind of death.

He thought of the gun he'd hidden on the top shelf of his closet. Maybe it was time he go to his house to retrieve it. Maybe it was time he started carrying it with him at all times to make sure nobody ever got close to Julie again.

Hell, he was no hero. Every decision he'd made lately had been particularly unheroic because it had been made to serve only him. He didn't care about himself anymore. He didn't care if the police somehow managed to link him to McDowell's death. He didn't give a damn if he spent time in jail. All he cared about was keeping Julie safe.

If he was caught with the gun on him, he had no idea what might happen. He had no idea if the gun had a history that would lead him straight to jail. That no longer mattered. The only thing that mattered was that he needed to protect Julie through this deadly threat.

He certainly couldn't rely on the police to do anything. They were as clueless as he and Julie were in this madness. His thoughts were interrupted as he heard her coming back down the stairs.

Despite the trauma she'd been through, she looked beautiful in a short, soft pink robe. She walked to the sofa and melted down onto the cushion next to him.

The scent of minty soap and spring flowers wafted from her as she snuggled against his side as if she belonged there. She believed she belonged there. He couldn't help but put his arm around her and hold her close.

It was amazing to him that she had accepted him so readily in her life. Without any memories of him, she had taken his word for it that they were engaged. She'd just assumed she loved him and he loved her. Such trust humbled him.

"I always feel so safe in your arms," she said with a deep sigh.

"I want you to be safe always," he replied.

She raised her head to look at him and he saw her need there. She needed him and tonight he needed her. He had a feeling the end was quickly approaching and when it slammed into them he would not only crush her world, but he'd wind up back in that dark space of loneliness and pain once again.

Chapter Twelve

Julie awoke in Nick's arms. His naked body was spooned close to hers and his arm was flung around her. Dawn light barely crept into the window and the last thing she wanted to do was to think of moving from this place of feeling so blissfully loved.

Their lovemaking the night before had been wonderful, but with a touch of desperation. It had begun slow and gentle, then had quickly moved to fast and frantic. It was as if they'd both known there was no promise of tomorrow.

She frowned and closed her eyes once again as thoughts of those horrifying moments in the pawn shop with her potential killer raced through her mind.

Her ankle ached with the memory of his tight fist wrapped around it. Her throat threatened to close up as she remembered his hands squeezing her.

Who on earth wanted to kill her? And why? What could she possibly know that was worth her death? She couldn't imagine even possessing a secret that big—that important—to somebody else. She worked in a pawn shop, for crying out loud. She wasn't the type to get involved in anything illegal.

But apparently she did possess a secret that threatened somebody else. And that somebody wanted her silenced forever.

Damn, she'd forgotten her cell phone. Now she'd have to drive back to work to get it. The memory of that night began to replay in her mind again, this time with more vivid detail.

THE NIGHT AIR had been hot as she'd driven to the shop. Her car air conditioner had barely started to cut through the heat when she arrived. Clouds had chased away the moonshine, making the night darker than usual.

She hurried from her car to the back door and breathed a sigh of relief as she went into the shop's coolness. She flipped on the light in the office and spied her cell phone right where she'd left it, but just after she grabbed it, the back door flew open and she heard the sound of a man laughing.

The laughter stopped abruptly as she stepped out of the office and saw...

DAMMIT. The memory flew away and she released a sigh of frustration.

Nick's arm tightened around her. "Are you all right?" His sleep-deepened voice filled her with pleasant warmth.

"I'm okay. Go back to sleep. It's still early."

He stroked her arm for a moment and then she knew he was asleep again. She was so lucky to have this man in her life. It was the last thought she had before she took her own advice and fell back to sleep.

She awakened to bright sunshine dancing through the curtains and she was alone in the bed. She rolled over on her back and stared up at the ceiling.

A wave of memories poured into her head…flashes of visions that filled some of the holes in her mind with missing information.

A lunch at a favorite Chinese restaurant with Casey…an argument with Max at work…and Tony telling her he wanted out of the family business.

The memories continued to assault her brain…her mother and father telling all the siblings that they were moving out of the family home…her shopping online for a coral-colored vase for her bedroom.

They were vignettes of a life, nothing earth-shattering, but they filled her with a huge relief. It was as if a dam had broken and assured her that sooner rather than later everything would come back to her.

What hadn't come back to her were any memories of Nick or anything having to do with why somebody might want her dead. Still, she was eager to share with him what had just happened. She wanted to tell him about the flood of memories that had suddenly come back to her.

She got out of bed and pulled on her robe, then working her fingers through her hair she headed down the stairs. As always, the scent of coffee greeted her and she found Nick at the kitchen table with a cup of the fresh brew in front of him.

Despite the fact that she'd made love to him the night before, a wild tingling swept through her body at the sight of him. He wore only a pair of jeans. His hair was slightly mussed and he gave her a sleepy smile as she entered the room.

"You look like you just rolled out of bed," she said and moved to the counter to pour herself a cup of coffee.

"I could say the same about you," he replied. They shared a smile and then she joined him at the table.

"Guess what?"

"What?"

How she loved that lazy smile of his. "I was just lying in bed and suddenly a ton of memories came back to me."

He sat straighter in his chair. "What kind of memories?"

"Just things I did over the past ten months… fairly boring, mundane things like having lunch out with my sister and Joel telling me about his new puppy. Unfortunately no memories of you or why somebody wants to kill me appeared. But at least it's a start, right?"

"Right," he replied.

"It seems like I didn't remember the very best and the very worst that happened in that missing time." She smiled at him again. "The best of course being our meeting and falling in love. The worst, whatever secret I supposedly know that's worth killing me for."

"And I hope you remember those things quickly," he replied.

She took a sip of her coffee and then frowned at him thoughtfully. "You know, it's like a song title that's on the very tip of your tongue and the harder you try to remember it, the more elusive it becomes."

"What were you thinking about when the memories came back to you?"

"I was thinking about last night and how good we are together. We are good, aren't we?" She held her breath as she waited for him to answer. Just because she thought their love-making was magical didn't mean he felt the same way.

He released a small laugh. "Julie, we're better than good together."

"Why did you laugh?"

"Because you never fail to amaze me with your complete openness," he replied.

"Is that good or bad?" she asked.

"It's wonderfully refreshing and good."

She warmed beneath the smile he gave her. "You know what sounds good to me? Bacon and eggs. I know you aren't much of a breakfast eater, but I'm in the mood for some crispy bacon and a cheese omelet. What do you think?"

"I wouldn't turn up my nose at that. What can I do to help?"

"Absolutely nothing. Just sit there and look totally hot and handsome," she replied and then laughed. "Mr. Simon, I do believe I just saw a blush sweep across your face."

He grinned. "You make me blush when you say stuff like that. That's what I was talking about, you're just so open and up-front with your feelings."

"And that's one of the things you love about me, right?"

He laughed and then sobered. "Yeah, that's one of the things I love about you."

Her heart swelled with happiness and she got up from the table. "Just for that, I'm going to make you bacon and the best omelet you've ever had."

Julie got to work. She hoped if she kept herself busy all day she wouldn't think about the terror of the night before. By doing mundane chores maybe her mind would fill in the rest of the memories she lacked and so desperately needed.

Breakfast was pleasant and she imagined it was what it would always be like once she and Nick got married. She felt like she was already married to him. However, she also knew that the twenty-four-hour-a-day relationship they shared now wasn't reality.

Reality was them each going to their own jobs in the morning and then being together once again in the evening. But reality was also his face being the first one she saw in the morning and the last one she saw before she fell asleep in his arms.

She wanted to get back to a normal life, whatever that had been before her accident. She was sure Nick was also eager to get some normalcy back in his life, as well.

More than anything she wanted a ring on her finger from him. She wanted to talk to him about wedding venues and flowers and wedding cakes. She wanted to plan the ceremony that would make her Nick's bride.

It was just after two o'clock in the afternoon when her sister called.

"Mom and I want to take you out to dinner tonight," Casey said. "And don't give me any excuses. We aren't going to take no for an answer. After what you went through last night, we want—we need—a girls' night out."

Julie didn't want to go. What she wanted was to spend the evening watching movies or whatever with Nick. She wanted to snuggle up against him on the sofa, where she felt safe and loved, and watch a silly movie that made them laugh.

"Casey, I really don't—"

"I said we won't take no for an answer." Casey cut in. "Julie, we need to see you and assure ourselves you're really okay. From what Daddy told us, you had a terrible experience last night. It will just be for a little while. I promise we'll get you home early."

Julie looked over at Nick, who was watching one of his football tapes on the television. "Do you mind if I go out to dinner this evening with my mom and sister?"

"Are you sure you feel up to it?" he asked. She nodded and he continued. "Then while you're gone I'll head over to my place to grab a few more things."

"Okay," Julie said back into the phone. "Just tell me what time and I'll be ready."

With plans made for Casey to pick her up at six, Julie went upstairs to do a little cleaning while Nick continued to watch the tapes and make notes on a notepad.

Before Julie knew it the day was gone and it was time to shower and get dressed for the night out. She didn't feel like going, but she knew her mother probably wanted to see for herself that Julie was fine after the ordeal she'd gone through last night.

Physically she was fine, but the thought of leaving the house caused more than a little bit of surprising anxiety to ripple through her, which was specifically why she was forcing herself to go. She didn't want to wind up agoraphobic, afraid to leave this safe space of her home for fear danger would come to her. She should be perfectly fine with her mother and sister.

At five to six she came downstairs and moved to the front door to watch for Casey. Nick joined her at the door. "That red dress looks gorgeous on you. You look way too nice to be going out without me," he said.

"I could say the same about you," she countered. Tucked into his white shorts was a short-sleeved, button-up, hunter-green shirt that popped the green color of his eyes.

"When am I going to get to see your house?" she asked. "I know I've been there before, but since I don't have any memories of it, I'd like to see it again." She wanted to see the space he called home. You could tell a lot about people by the things they surrounded themselves with.

"We can go tomorrow if you want," he replied.

A honk sounded from the driveway. She rolled her eyes. "I'm sure she sees me standing right here but she has a horn fetish."

He grinned at her. "I can think of worse fetishes to have."

She laughed. "Now, how about you give me a goodbye kiss that curls my toes?" She leaned into him.

He gazed at her for a long moment, his eyes going darker, and then he placed his lips over hers. His lips were soft and warm and made her want to stay home to make love with him all night long.

All too quickly he pulled away from her. He shoved an errant strand of her hair away from her cheek. "Have fun and be safe," he said.

She smiled. "With my mother and sister by my side, nothing and nobody would dare try to get to me. I'll be fine and I'll see you later. Casey promised me it would be an early night."

Despite all the bad things that had happened since her accident, her heart was light as she left the porch. Everything with Nick felt so easy, so good. Although they hadn't talked about their engagement and plans for a wedding since her car wreck, she knew those things were definitely in her future.

She frowned as she reached the car and realized her mother wasn't inside. She opened the door and slid into the passenger seat. "Where's Mom?"

Casey put the car in Reverse. "She and Dad went out to some farmhouse close to Smithville to look at some antiques. We're supposed to pick her up there."

Julie laughed. "Which means we're riding to her rescue. You know how long Dad can take when he's negotiating for more stuff."

"Forever," Casey replied. She shot a quick look at Julie. "How are you doing after last night? I heard about you being attacked."

Julie had tried all day long not to think about what had happened the night before. Even now in the safety of Casey's car an icy chill threatened to overwhelm her. The back of her throat tightened as she remembered the man's hands wrapped around her neck. She'd used makeup to dust across the faint bruises that had appeared.

"I'm fine," she replied. "I really don't want

to talk about it. I don't even want to think about it."

"And you really don't know why somebody is after you?"

"I really don't, although my memories are coming back and I think it won't be long before I'll know exactly what's going on."

"That's great. Maybe then you'll remember that you borrowed my cute pink blouse with the white cuffs and you'll return it to me."

Julie laughed. "Okay, I'll get that back to you as soon as you return my favorite winter boots."

Once again Casey glanced at Julie and then returned her attention to the narrow highway. "I borrowed those boots in ninth grade," she protested.

"And I've never forgiven you for not returning them to me," Julie replied with a grin. Casey laughed and a surge of love for her sister welled up inside Julie.

Sure, Casey was flighty and irresponsible. She was spoiled and could be petulant, but she could also be such fun to be around.

Julie cast her gaze out the front car window. A plethora of trees stood tall and thick some distance away on either side of the road. That was one of the things Julie loved about

Kansas City. Within a fifteen-minute drive from the northern suburbs you could be out in the middle of nowhere.

Even though the highway was just a two-lane, there was plenty of traffic since it led to a lake where many families enjoyed boating and other summer fun.

"I'd ask how you and Nick are getting along, but from the slobbery kiss I saw you two share before you left the house, I would guess that everything must be going great," Casey said.

Julie laughed once again. "It wasn't slobbery and everything is better than great. I just wish I could remember all the time I've lost with him."

"Too bad there isn't a drug you could take that would instantly restore all the rest of those memories," Casey replied.

Every muscle in Julie's body tensed. *Drugs. A large box of prescription bottles.* She closed her eyes as the memories suddenly assaulted her.

She'd been in the office to retrieve her cell phone…

THE BACK DOOR opened and male laughter echoed up the small hallway. She peeked her head out of the office and saw a large, young man with bulky, tattooed arms carrying a large box. His bald head gleamed in the light overhead and his eyes widened in surprise when he saw her.

JULIE'S EYES FLEW OPEN, but still the memories came.

Casey stepping up behind the man with a box of pill bottles in her arms...

Julie looking at the bottles in the box... OxyContin. Oxycodone. Xanax. And others, probably even street drugs. They'd been selling them outside the back of the shop at night...

Julie'd had a rough idea what those kind of drugs would fetch on the street and remembered thinking that Casey and her boyfriend Ace had to be raking in big bucks.

"Don't tell!" Casey had screamed at her. "Just get the hell out of here now and forget what you saw."

Julie had left, but there'd been no way she wasn't going to tell. Casey and her boyfriend were not only doing something illegal, they were also jeopardizing everything her family had all worked for. If those two were caught selling dope out of the pawn shop, then it was possible the whole place could be shut down.

When Julie left the pawn shop on that terrible night, Casey had followed her. Julie had never seen her sister so out of control, so enraged, as she'd confronted Julie in Julie's living room. That night Casey's eyes had shone with lethal intent. When Casey had physically attacked her, Julie had thrown the candle at her and then run outside and jumped in her car.

Danger.

It rang in the air inside the car. It screamed inside Julie's head.

Keep your cool, a small voice whispered inside her.

"Dad sure dragged Mom a long way from town," Julie said, glad her voice didn't give away any of her inner turmoil. There was no way Julie now believed Casey was taking her to pick up their mother for a lovely dinner together.

Was she taking her to meet up with her boyfriend? The man Julie now was certain had been the one who had tried to kill her the night before.

She needed to get out of the car. She couldn't trust Casey. Last night had been a failed attempt to silence her forever. So, now where were they really going?

With terror crawling up the back of her throat, she considered her options. She only had one. She had to get out of the car.

She drew in a deep breath for courage, knowing she was taking a huge chance. She prayed she wouldn't wind up dead as she reached over and grabbed the steering wheel.

"What in the hell are you doing?" Casey screamed.

Julie fought for control and yanked the wheel as hard as she could toward her. The car careered off the road, dove down and then up the ditch, and finally rolled to a halt.

Julie didn't waste any time. She tore off her seat belt and shoved her door open. She took off running for the woods. It was only when a deep male voice yelled from someplace behind her that she slowed and threw a glance over her shoulder.

Her blood ran cold and she nearly stumbled in shocked surprise. Casey stood next to her car. The trunk was now open and running toward Julie was the bulky man who had tried to kill her the night before.

Oh, God…had she just played into their hands? Had this been their plan all along?

To get her out in the middle of nowhere and kill her?

The only choice she had now was to run like the wind and hope like hell she could find someplace to hide until somehow, someway, help would come. She desperately prayed that somebody else found her before her sister and her boyfriend did.

THERE WAS NO sense of homecoming when Nick walked through the front door of his house. He walked around, touching things he and Debbie had bought together and remembering the plans they'd once made for their future together.

The anger, the self-destructive rage, he'd dwelled in after her murder was gone, replaced by the normal sadness of loss. He would always remember his first wife, but right now he had another woman on his mind.

Julie. He'd nearly lost her last night to dark forces that remained buried in her mind. What had she seen? What did she know that now had her life at risk?

He walked into the master bedroom, turned on the television on the dresser and sank down onto the foot of the bed. Julie needed to get all her memories back.

The only times he didn't want her to remember anything was when he held her in his arms and when her eyes lit up with such love for him. Whenever they shared a kiss or made love, he didn't want her to remember that she had never met him before the night of the accident.

She needed to remember that she'd never loved him.

He saw no happy ending for them. But he desperately wanted a happy ending for her. He wanted the danger gone and Julie free to live her life…to find love and move forward with her dreams.

Again a sadness gripped his soul, especially as he thought of her with another man. Maybe this was his penance for entering into an agreement that would celebrate six men's murders.

There was no way he believed Julie would forgive him when she learned the truth. He'd not only pretended to be her fiancé, he'd made up a whole history that was nothing but a fantasy to serve his own needs.

She wouldn't remember that he'd held her when she'd been frightened during a thunderstorm. She wouldn't care that he'd been there for her through her laughter and her tears.

He'd built a past with her based on lies. He'd also made love to her under those false pretenses. Who in the hell would want to build a future with a man like him?

When she'd opened her beautiful eyes after the accident, she'd taken all that he'd told her at face value. She had openly and trustingly given him everything…her body, her heart and her soul.

He loved her. He loved that she had little self-edit when it came to what thoughts she expressed out loud. He adored her sense of humor and how often they laughed together about the silliest thing.

Yes, he loved her with every fiber of his being. He wanted his future to be with her, but his feelings didn't matter. He could love her to the moon and back, but he knew she was going to hate him when the truth came out.

He got up from the bed and walked over to his closet. If he couldn't be with her forever, he could at least keep her safe until her memories returned.

He reached up on the closet's top shelf and pulled down the hoodie wrapped around the weapon.

Once again, the gun felt cold and alien in

his grip. It wasn't that he didn't know how to handle one. He and a couple of the other coaches occasionally went to a gun range to shoot. Yes, he knew his way around the weapon, but it was how and why he'd gotten this particular gun that made it feel like it didn't belong in his hand.

He grabbed a small duffel from the bottom of the closet. He placed the gun in the bottom and then folded several T-shirts and placed them on top.

Glancing at the clock, he noted that it was time for the evening news. He figured he still had a couple of hours before Julie would be back home, so he placed the duffel on the bed and once again sat down.

He'd been trying to catch the news every evening to see if there had been any follow-up to Brian McDowell's murder. However, each day the news was filled with other murders and crimes, making it impossible for him to follow the investigation. He also watched the news to see if any of the other men on their hit list had been killed.

How he wished he could rewrite the history of the past year. How he wished he would have really met Julie in a coffee shop and everything he'd told her about their relationship was real.

His attention was captured by a picture on the television. He grabbed the remote and turned up the volume.

"Police have been called to the scene of an accident along 169 Highway. Eyewitnesses say a car spun out of control and a woman jumped out and ran into the wooded area. Two other car occupants also abandoned the car and ran. This video was shot by a bystander."

The blond newscaster disappeared and a shaky video came on showing a car on the side of the road and a woman in a red dress jumping out of the passenger seat.

It was a brief clip but Nick's blood stopped flowing through his veins. A tight pressure filled his chest. That was Casey's car and it had been Julie who had run away. He didn't know exactly what was happening, but he knew with certainty she needed him...now!

He grabbed the duffel bag and raced out of the house.

Once he was on the road, questions began swirling through his head. What was going on? Why would Julie get out of the car and run away from the scene? From her sister and her mother? It didn't make sense.

She would only do that if she believed she was in immediate danger. Casey? Their mother? He couldn't imagine one of them being the source of the threat, but he knew in his gut Julie was in a wealth of trouble.

He thought of the gun he carried with him. He would have no problem putting a bullet into somebody who was trying to hurt Julie. He didn't give a damn who they were.

All he had to do was to get to her in time.

Chapter Thirteen

Julie's heart nearly beat out of her chest as she ran through the thick woods. A thrashing came from someplace behind her, letting her know her sister and Ace were coming after her.

The sweltering late-evening heat made it even more difficult for her to catch her breath as she frantically looked around for someplace to hide.

Brush and thickets tried to trip her up, grabbing at her legs and catching on her dress. Damn her choice of a red dress. It was like a vivid target in the green depths of the woods.

She had no idea where she was going. All that was important at the moment was that Ace not catch her. There was no question in her mind that if he caught her, he'd kill her.

He'd already tried once and, if he had his way, she wouldn't make it out of these woods.

Gasping for air, she ducked behind a tree to catch her breath.

"Julie…come out," Casey called from someplace in the distance. "We don't want to hurt you. We just want to talk to you. Come out so we can have an adult conversation about things."

Julie squeezed her eyes tightly closed against the tears that threatened to fall. She didn't believe Casey. Her sister had probably been in the pawn shop when Ace had tried to strangle her. It had probably been Casey who had turned out the lights. Nobody who wanted to have a conversation with you hid their killer boyfriend in the car trunk.

She stuffed down the sense of betrayal, shoved the utter devastation away. She couldn't deal with that right now. She had more important things on her mind, like trying to stay alive.

"Come on, Julie. I promise everything is going to be okay. Just talk to us for a few minutes and then we can all go out to eat and we'll take you back home," Casey said in a smooth, reassuring voice.

Julie wasn't reassured. The woman attempting to get Julie out of her hiding place had nothing to do with the sister Julie had grown up with. She had no idea what had changed Casey, and right now she didn't care.

"Julie…" The deep male whisper seemed to come from right behind her.

Too close. He was far too close. With a gasp, she took off running again. She ran as fast as she could, blinded by tears and terror. She cried out as she stumbled over a tree root and fell to the ground.

She jumped up and cast a quick glance behind her.

Ace was visible and as he saw her he raised an arm. Was that a gun in his hand?

Drawing in a deep gulp of air, she dove to her right and rolled until she came to another big tree. She crawled on her hands and knees to get behind it.

A siren sounded from the direction of where she'd run from the car. Thank goodness, help was arriving. Still, she couldn't exactly dash out into the open to get to the police. The siren wailed for another minute and then went silent.

She remained plastered against the tree trunk, holding her breath and praying Ace hadn't seen where she'd rolled when she'd hit the ground. Still, no police officer would know where she was unless she let them know.

A rustle sounded far too close to her. Drawing in another deep breath, she released a scream that sent birds flying from the tops of the trees. And then she ran again.

Once again she darted ahead blindly, just wanting to keep one step ahead of Ace. She tried to weave a path that would take her back toward the highway where hopefully police had arrived and could save her.

However, she'd become disoriented and, without the sound of the siren, wasn't sure in which direction to run. Again she leaned her back against a tree trunk, her gaze shooting frantically all around.

How long had it been since she'd run from the car? Minutes? An hour? It felt like forever. Nick. Her heart cried out his name.

How she wished his strong, loving arms were around her right now. She needed him. She frowned, her mind racing for more memories…any memories of him.

A strong hand grabbed her wrist and she screamed as she was pulled away from the tree and the tight hold released. "Hands up."

She stared into the barrel of a gun, a police officer's gun. "Oh, thank God," she exclaimed to the middle-aged man clad in a khaki uniform. "They were going to kill me. They didn't want me to tell what I knew. At first I didn't remember what I saw, but my memories all came back and they want to kill me…"

She knew she was babbling, but she couldn't stop herself. "He was hiding in the trunk. Ace…my sister's boyfriend…he was in the trunk of her car. My sister told me we were going out to dinner, but they were taking me someplace to kill me." A deep sob escaped her.

"We'll get everything sorted out, ma'am," the officer said as he holstered his gun. "Right now, I need you to keep your hands up over your head and walk that way." He gestured for her to walk to her left.

She walked in front of him for some distance and finally they broke out of the woods.

She froze as she saw Casey and Ace standing next to Casey's car with two other officers.

"Why aren't they in handcuffs?" she asked. "They wanted to kill me. They need to be arrested."

"Julie, come on, honey. Everything is going to be okay," Casey called.

"Jules, we were just going for a nice drive," Ace said as if they were the best friends in the world.

Jules? What in the hell were they playing at? A hundred knots twisted in her stomach as the officer moved her forward.

Casey leaned toward the officer standing next to her and spoke, but Julie was too far away to hear the conversation.

Still, the look the officer gave her was full of speculation.

Casey, who could charm the bark off a tree. What had she been telling the officers about Julie? What lies had she told them to save her and her boyfriend's asses?

"Julie, everything is going to be okay," Casey said when Julie reached the car. "You're safe now." Her voice was filled with such caring, but her eyes held a hard edge Julie had never seen before.

"I understand you were recently in a car accident, Ms. Peterson." The officer next to Casey was a big man and he wore a name tag that identified him as Deputy Ben Rodman.

"What does that have to do with anything?" she asked defensively.

"Julie, you know you haven't been yourself since the accident," Casey replied. She looked at all the policemen. "We've all been so very worried about her."

"We thought she might enjoy a nice drive, but she freaked out and grabbed the wheel and then bailed from the car," Ace said.

"Shut up." Julie snapped at him. "You were hiding in the trunk for a reason. I don't even know you and you tried to kill me last night in the pawn shop."

The big, bald man shook his head with a sad smile. "Now, Julie, you know that isn't true." He looked at the deputy who had brought Julie back. "She's been paranoid since her car wreck and thinks her family members are out to kill her."

They were trying to make her look crazy and, by the expressions on the officers' faces, it was working.

"He's lying and what I told you is the truth," she replied frantically. "Check it out with the police department in Kansas City. I was attacked last night and it was because they don't want me telling anyone they've been selling drugs out of the back of the family business."

"Julie." Casey shook her head in obvious pity.

"You've got to believe me," Julie exclaimed. Tears burned at her eyes. "They were taking me someplace to kill me so I couldn't tell anyone about what they've been doing."

"She needs mental help," Casey said. "My family has been talking about having her committed for a little while so she can get the help she needs."

Julie gasped. This was all going so horribly wrong. "He had a gun," she said and pointed to Ace. "I saw it. He pointed it at me and was going to shoot me."

"Julie, honey, the deputies patted down Ace. There's no gun," Casey replied as if she were speaking to a three-year-old.

Julie looked at each of the deputies' faces. Oh, God, they believed Casey and Ace's story. She was in big trouble. It was possible she'd wind up in some mental hospital and nobody would ever believe her about what Casey and Ace had been doing…what they had already done.

At that moment a familiar car screeched to

a halt behind one of the police cars and Nick got out. She'd never been so happy to see somebody before in her entire life.

"Nick!" Before anyone could stop her, she ran to him. His arms awaited her and enfolded her tight. His heart beat against hers in the same frantic rhythm.

"Are you all right?" He pulled slightly away from her as his gaze bore into hers.

"They're trying to make it look like I'm crazy. They were taking me someplace to kill me, Nick." Before she could say anything more, Deputy Rodman joined them. "This is my fiancé, Nick Simon. He can tell you what's going on. He'll tell you I'm not crazy."

Rodman held up his hand. "We're taking you all in to the station to sort this out."

Nick released her. "I'll follow you there."

Minutes later Julie was in the back of a police cruiser and her sister and Ace were passengers in another vehicle. Fear still tightened her muscles and dried her mouth.

Were they going to let Casey and Ace go? She wanted them locked up. Her heart not only ached for the little sister she'd loved, but also for her parents, who would be devastated by Casey's crimes.

IT WAS HOURS later when Nick and Julie finally walked out of the police station. Ace was being held for pending charges and two outstanding warrants. Casey was also under arrest. A search of her car had uncovered a box of prescription pills not prescribed to her.

Julie slid into the passenger seat of Nick's car and leaned her head back as Nick got in behind the wheel and started the engine.

"Tired?" he asked.

"Mentally and physically exhausted," she replied. She looked down at her dress. Pulls and tears in the material evidenced her mad dash through the woods. Thank God, her dress's was the only death that had occurred today.

She pulled her cell phone from her purse and stared down at her parents' number. "I need to call Mom and Dad and tell them what's happened. This is going to absolutely break their hearts."

"It would have broken their hearts if Casey and Ace had succeeded in killing you," Nick replied. His voice deepened as he continued. "It definitely would have broken mine."

She flashed him a grateful glance and then hit the button on her phone that would connect her with her parents. It was the most difficult conversation she'd ever had.

She cried. Her mother cried and her father cursed. They were in shock, but ultimately they proclaimed their love for Julie and the fact that Casey would now have to face the consequences of her actions.

"Are you sure you're all right?" her mother asked.

"I'm fine," she replied. "I'm with Nick and I'm okay. I'm just tired and ready for my life to get back to normal."

By the time the call had ended, she was utterly drained. Once again she leaned her head back and closed her eyes. The memories she'd been missing again flashed through her mind.

Difficult customers in the shop... Joel's new dog... Casey and Ace coming in the back door with drugs... Casey attacking her in her living room, breaking the lamp while Julie threw the candle, hitting the glass on the painting and, finally, her jumping into her car to escape.

She opened her eyes and sat straighter as Nick came to a stop in her driveway. Her heart started a new quickened pace, one of disquiet...of uncertainty mingling with a faint touch of fear.

She looked at Nick in the purple shadows of twilight that had descended. He had been by her side through everything. She was desperately in love with him, but at the moment that didn't matter.

"I've been desperately searching my memory to find you and I realize now that my memories of you aren't missing. They were never there to begin with. You aren't my fiancé, so who in the hell are you?"

NICK HAD WAITED for this moment to happen. Initially he'd anticipated it and then he had dreaded it. Now it was upon him and a swell of desperation filled his chest.

"Can we go inside and talk?" he asked.

Her eyes were dark and filled with mistrust. She gave a curt nod of her head and then, together, they exited the car and walked to the front door. At least she wasn't locking him out before she could hear his side of the story.

Her shoulders were stiff, her beautiful face emotionless as they went inside and sat on opposite sides of the sofa. Only able to imagine the trauma she'd been through as she'd run for her life through the woods, the only thing he really wanted to do was to hold her close and assure himself she was really okay. However, everything about her posture let him know she wouldn't welcome any kind of touch from him.

"Who are you and why are you in my life?" she asked.

"I'm the man who is in love with you," he replied.

She raised a trembling hand. "Don't. I know you weren't in the car with me on the night of the accident. I also know you and I didn't have a fight in my living room.

"Casey and I fought that night and I got into my car alone. Why are you here and where did you come from?" Her gaze searched his features as if she'd never seen him before this moment.

Where did he begin? How did he even start to try to make her understand what he had done? He was desperate to get her to believe that none of that mattered, that he was in love with her now and that he believed she'd fallen in love with him.

"I was on the street when you wrecked your car. I'm the one who called for help," he said.

She stared at him without blinking, obviously waiting for him to make sense of things.

What had made sense to him on the night of her accident now seemed completely insane.

"So, how did you go from Good Samaritan to my fiancé?" she asked.

His chest ached with regret. He averted his gaze, unable to look at her and tell her about all of his elaborate lies.

"I was at the wrong place at the wrong time that night."

As he thought about his intentions and the reason he'd been on the street, it felt as if it had all happened in a nightmare or to somebody else.

"You were unconscious in the car and I made an impromptu decision to pretend to be your fiancé. I only intended to pretend until you got medical help, but then the responding officer took me to the hospital and I couldn't tell him I'd lied to him about our relationship. Then you regained consciousness and believed I was your fiancé, and I only intended to continue the pretense until you came home."

"You use the word 'pretense.' Call it what it was, you lied." Her harsh tone made him look at her again.

Her arms were folded tight across her chest

and looking at her caused a new pressure to build inside him. Her eyes were bright with anger, but her lips trembled with a vulnerability that spoke of pain.

He nodded. "My initial impromptu lie spun way out of control. When I brought you here and saw the damage in the room, I knew you might be in some kind of trouble. I didn't want to tell you the truth then. You got that threatening phone call and I didn't want to bow out of your life."

He leaned forward. "Julie, our relationship started with my lie, but it became real to me. I'm in love with you. I don't just want you to be my pretend fiancée, I want you to be my wife."

A laugh escaped her. A bitter sound that shot a sharp arrow into his heart. "I don't know you. I don't know what all you lied about. I don't even know if your name is really Nick Simon or not."

"That really is my name and I really am a high school physical ed teacher and coach. I didn't lie about who I am, and the feelings I have for you are very real."

He couldn't stand it any longer. He had to touch her. He scooted closer to her and tried to ignore how she stiffened at his nearness.

He reached out a hand toward her, but she jumped up off the sofa before he could make any contact.

"You allowed me to make love with you without telling me you were a stranger in my life." For the first time, tears glinted in her eyes. "You let me fall in love with you, knowing all of it was a lie."

"But that part wasn't a lie," he protested. "What I feel for you is real and, if you look deep in your heart, I know you'll realize the love you feel for me is just as real."

She swiped at a tear that trekked down her cheek then raised her fingers to her temple and rubbed. "I need you to leave."

He stood. "Julie, don't throw this all away. I'm sorry. I'm so damned sorry about everything." A simmering desperation filled him. He had a feeling that if he left here tonight it would be the end of any hope he had to have her in his future. "I love you, Julie, and I need you in my life."

"And I need you to go," she replied. She dropped her hand to her side and didn't meet his gaze. "I thought Casey's betrayal of me was the worst I'd ever know. But this…? You…have utterly gutted me."

He remained in place, willing her to look

at him again, but she kept her gaze averted as tears slowly oozed from her eyes. She looked broken and the fact that he was responsible for that ached in him.

"Please go," she said softly. "You can come back and get your things tomorrow or the next day. And leave my house key on the table."

Dammit, he didn't want to leave. He wanted to pull her into his arms, somehow make her see that they were meant to be together forever.

He hesitated for what felt like a lifetime, a wealth of pain stabbing his heart. Then, with deep resignation, he pulled his key ring from his pocket. The silence between them was deafening as he took her house key off and laid it on the coffee table.

"It would have been so much easier if we'd really met in a coffee shop a year ago," she said softly. She finally met his gaze and in the depths of her eyes was the darkness of pain, of betrayal so great it stole his breath away.

He thought about her words and released a heavy sigh. "Julie, I wasn't a good enough man for you a year ago."

He hoped she'd stop him as he walked toward the front door, but she didn't. He held on to a modicum of hope until he stepped out the door and heard it slam and lock behind him.

Would he get an opportunity to talk to her tomorrow? Or would she pack his things and place them on the front porch? At least he was leaving with the knowledge that she was safe now, although there would certainly be emotional fallout from Casey's actions.

Fighting against the wave of heartache that threatened to consume him, he got into his car. He'd been a fool to think she would be able to easily forgive him. He'd been completely delusional to ever believe there would be a happy ending in this.

Now he was left with a fiery love for a woman he'd probably never have in his life and a gun he didn't want in his glove box. At least he could do something about the gun.

It was representative of the man he had been, an angry animal who had lost all of his humanity and dignity to grief. He wasn't that person anymore and he couldn't ever imagine becoming that person again, no matter what happened in his future.

He headed north, his headlights cutting through the darkness of night. He couldn't go home before getting rid of the gun. It was the last piece that tied him to a dark past.

As he drove, his head replayed each and every moment he'd shared with Julie. She'd helped him not only get his sense of humor back, but also his passion.

He'd looked forward each morning to getting up and spending time with her. He'd wanted to be there with her for all the good times and the bad.

A hollow wind blew through him as the landscape in front of him washed out like a watercolor painting. He wiped the sudden, unexpected tears from his eyes.

He passed the spot on the highway where Casey's car had been parked and the woods where Julie had run for her life. Thank God, at least the danger to her would be no more.

She'd been so closed off from him. He clenched his hands more tightly around the steering wheel. Could he really blame her?

He was guilty of wanting her enough to take her to bed, to make love to her. He was guilty of lying to her over and over again about the little things that made up a real life, only in this case it had been a false life that he'd invented.

He turned onto a narrow road with thick trees on either side. This road would take him to an old dock on the big lake north of the city.

Although he deeply regretted hurting Julie, it was difficult for him to regret the forces that had brought them together. He wouldn't take back a minute of his time with her. He would cherish the memories of loving her forever.

He reached a small parking area and pulled his car to a halt. He turned off his lights, then reached into the glove box and retrieved the gun and a small cleaning towel he kept there to occasionally wipe off his windshield.

As he got out of his car the hot, sultry night air quickly embraced him. He walked out onto the dock and sat at the edge. His father used to bring him fishing here when he was a young boy. Nick hadn't been back to this dock since his father and mother's death.

For a moment his head filled with happy memories of those times with his dad. If he'd had his parents' support when Debbie had been murdered, would he have walked the same path of rage and revenge? Probably not. But when that murder had occurred, he'd been all alone and ripe to fall in with the other men who were in the same mental hell.

Wiping down the weapon, his thoughts

turned to the five men in the pact. He assumed their plans would go forward and more deaths would occur. He wished he could make them understand that the way to ease pain and heartache wasn't murder but was, instead, love.

It sounded like a damn cliché, but maintaining that kind of rage for any length of time only ate up your insides and made it impossible to move on. No amount of vengeance would bring back their loved ones.

In any case, the pact no longer mattered. He was out. He would never see those men again unless it was a chance meeting at the grocery store or on the street.

With the gun carefully wiped down, he stood. This was the last thing that tied him to a killing rage, to a darkness he knew he'd never plunge into again.

Drawing a deep breath, he threw the gun into the water. He knew from those days of fishing with his father that this particular area was filled with crappie beds. He hoped the gun would tangle so tightly in them that it would never be found again.

The moon overhead was big and bright, reflecting on the water that occasionally rippled with fish or insects. For the first time since arriving, he became aware of the cacophony of sound that surrounded him. Insects clicked and whirred and the deep bass croaking of a bullfrog filled the air.

As his thoughts returned to Julie, burning tears blurred his vision. He'd never wanted anything as badly as he wanted her. He sank back down to sit on the dock and allowed his tears to run free. The ball was now in her court and he had the terrible feeling that she'd never be able to forgive him.

Chapter Fourteen

Nick.

Julie woke with his name on her lips and tears in her eyes. The heartache that rocked through her was definitely more painful than the bruises and scratches she'd sustained from her ordeal the day before.

Minutes later she stood beneath a hot shower and tried to halt the seemingly endless supply of tears she had. She told herself she was weeping because her knees and elbows were bruised by her tumble over the tree root.

Every muscle in her body ached from her exertions the night before. Her own sister had wanted her dead. She had plenty to cry about, but she couldn't fool herself. This morning her tears were solely for the loss of Nick.

Last night after he'd left she'd cried for hours, not knowing if she was crying because of Nick's betrayal or Casey's. She'd never felt so alone.

He loves you, a little voice whispered inside her as she dressed for the day. But did he really? How could she accept words of love from a man who had lied to her so many times about so many things?

It was funny…she'd believed herself madly in love with him the minute she'd been told that her fiancé was in the waiting room at the hospital. She hadn't questioned that love the entire time they'd been together. Even though she couldn't remember him, she'd fallen in love with him all over again.

He'd stood by her side through the worst things that would ever happen in her life. He'd done his best to protect her from danger when he could have just walked away.

She was so confused. But the one thing she wasn't confused about was the fact that she was madly and deeply in love with Nick.

She'd just sat to have a cup of coffee when a knock fell on her door. Her heartbeat accelerated. Was Nick here to get his things already? She wasn't ready to face him yet. She was still sorting out her emotions where he was concerned.

When a second knock sounded, this one

louder than the last, she reluctantly got out of her chair and hurried to answer. She didn't know if she was glad or disappointed that it was her mother.

"Mom," she said in surprise. Her surprise went to shock when her mother pulled her into a tight embrace. It had been years since Julie had been really hugged by Lynetta.

She finally released Julie and cleared her throat. "I smell fresh coffee."

"I was just sitting down for a cup," Julie replied.

A few moments later they were both seated at the table. "I had to come by and check on you," Lynetta said. "I'm so sorry for what you went through last night. Your father and I feel partially responsible."

Julie looked at her in surprise. "It isn't your fault."

"We've always been too easy on Casey. We didn't discipline her like we did everyone else and she chose the wrong paths and the wrong people."

Lynetta appeared older today than Julie had ever seen her.

"We spoiled her rotten and when we tried to cut the financial ties, she chose the easy path." Lynetta shook her head. "I still can't believe they were selling drugs out of the pawn shop."

"I'm sorry, Mom."

Lynetta quickly covered Julie's hand with hers. "There is absolutely no reason for you to apologize for anything. What Casey did was beyond inexcusable, first by selling drugs out of the shop and then in driving you someplace where that man could kill you." Her face paled. "I don't know what we would have done if they'd been successful and we'd lost you."

"You would have been able to hire somebody to work at the shop and take care of the books," Julie replied.

Her mother stared at her for a long moment and then anger flashed from her eyes. "Is that what you believe about us? That we only care about you because you're a good worker?"

Lynetta's eyes filled with tears and she squeezed Julie's hand. "Oh, honey, if that's what you believe, then your father and I have really messed up. I couldn't give a damn what you do or don't do in that shop. You're my daughter and all I've ever wanted was for you to be healthy and happy."

Julie burst into tears. Her mother's words soothed a part of her that had been wounded for a very long time. She finally pulled her hand from her mother's to wipe at the tears. "You have no idea how much I needed to hear that," she finally said when she regained control.

"Then I wish I would have told you that every single day of your life," Lynetta replied. "You're my firstborn daughter, Julie. I couldn't wait for you to be born. You filled a space in my heart that had been empty and you've made me very proud to be your mother every day of your life."

"I want to quit working at the shop." The words tumbled from Julie's mouth before she'd known she was going to say them. She held her breath to see how her mother would react.

Lynetta sat back in her chair, her features registering surprise.

Julie had been through a man chasing her around in the woods in an attempt to kill her. She'd also survived the man she loved telling her that love was built on lies. She suddenly felt strong enough to go after what she really wanted.

"I want to go back to school and get a nursing license," she said.

"A noble profession. Your father and I

would support you a hundred percent if that's what you want to do."

It was Julie's turn to be surprised. "I expected you to freak out and try to talk me out of quitting the shop."

"I told you, I want you happy, and if being a nurse is what makes you happy, then go for it. What does your fellow think about it?" Lynetta frowned. "As a matter of fact, where is Nick? I figured he'd be here with you today."

A renewed sense of pain speared through Julie. "We had a fight and he left last night."

"So, it was a serious fight?" Lynetta asked, and Julie nodded. "I hope you two work it out. I've never seen a man look at you with such love as Nick has when he looks at you."

"Really?" Julie stared at her mother intently.

"Really. That boy is head-over-heels in love with you. Trust me, your father sometimes still looks at me that way. That's the kind of love that will last a lifetime."

Julie couldn't help the way her heart swelled at her mother's words.

AN HOUR LATER she was still thinking about her conversation with her mother. She'd been both surprised and relieved by her mom's response to Julie telling her she wanted to quit working at the shop. She had definitely underestimated the love and support her parents had for her.

Was she also underestimating Nick's love for her? Was it possible she could get past all the lies he'd told her? Could she really believe his love was real when so many things had been pretend? She really didn't know.

There were questions she still needed to have answered. What had he been doing out on the street at midnight on the night of her accident? What, exactly, was true and what was false?

She didn't know where he lived. Did he really have a murdered wife? What about his parents? Had he lied about them being killed in a car accident?

Despite how angry she'd been with him, there was no question she couldn't imagine how she would have gotten through her ordeal without him.

He'd been there for her on the night of the horrible phone call and when the doll had been left for her to find. His arms had been the ones she'd wanted around her both on the night she'd been attacked in the pawn shop and yesterday when he'd pulled up behind the police car.

Why hadn't her heart told her immediately that he was a stranger? Even if her brain had malfunctioned with the amnesia, why hadn't her heart or instincts told her that their love wasn't real the moment he'd come into her hospital room?

The problem was…it didn't matter that she had no memories of him before her accident. Since that time she'd fallen helplessly in love with him.

She jumped as the phone rang. For just a brief moment she gazed at it in fear.

It's okay, a small voice whispered in her head. *The danger has passed.*

She answered.

"Julie?"

She squeezed her eyes tightly closed at the sound of his deep voice. "Yes?"

"Uh… I was wondering if now would be a good time for me to come over and get my things."

Her heartache deepened. He hadn't called to say he loved her. He hadn't called to tell her he couldn't live without her. He'd called to get his things.

"How about in an hour," she replied.

"That's good with me as long as it's good for you," he said.

"Then I'll see you in an hour." She quickly hung up the receiver and sank down on the sofa. She didn't know why she hadn't told him to come over right now.

But if she looked deeply into her heart, she knew the answer. As long as his items were in her house, she could pretend they were still a couple. When he picked up his clothing, the end of them would be final.

She got up from the sofa and walked upstairs. Instead of going down the hallway to her own bedroom, she veered into the guest room where he'd been staying.

One of his T-shirts lay on the bed. She picked it up and held it to her nose, breathing in the familiar scent of home and security.

The sight of a pair of his socks on the floor almost made her laugh as she remembered their conversation about his penchant for not picking up his socks. Instead, tears leaped into her eyes.

She threw the shirt back on the bed and angrily wiped at her tears. She was through crying over Nick Simon. It was time for her to start getting over him.

However, an hour later when the doorbell

rang, her heart leaped with the anticipation of seeing him again. Her hands trembled with nervous energy as she opened the door to him.

For a brief moment she couldn't speak. Oh, why did he have to look so wonderful in his jeans and a camo-green T-shirt that complemented the color of his eyes? Why did the mere sight of him threaten to break her heart all over again?

"Come in," she said quickly after an initial awkward pause. She opened the door further for him to enter. As he swept by her, his familiar scent wrapped around her broken heart. "Feel free to go upstairs to get your things," she said.

"Can we talk first?"

Once again she hesitated.

"Please, Julie," he said softly…pleadingly.

She gestured him toward the living room, although she wasn't sure they had anything to discuss. He'd used her until he didn't need her anymore and now he was here to take the last pieces of him away.

He walked into the living room and sank down on the sofa. She sat opposite him in a chair. There was no way she wanted to sit close to him. She didn't want to smell his familiar scent, feel the warmth of his body heat as he told her goodbye.

"Julie, I can't let this end like this," he said. He leaned forward, his eyes glittering bright and intent. "There's no question that initially I did you wrong. I made selfish choices that served only myself."

"Do you really have a wife who was murdered?"

"Absolutely. Why do you think I would lie about such a terrible thing?"

"The problem is I don't know what you lied about and what you didn't. What were you doing out on the street on the night of my accident?"

For the first time since they'd come into the living room, his gaze shifted away from her and to some point over her left shoulder.

He released a deep sigh. "If I tell you everything about that night then I'll be betraying the trust of five other men." His gaze met hers again. "I can promise you that I did nothing wrong and I can't regret what happened that night because it brought you to me."

Although he'd piqued her curiosity about the other men, she realized it didn't really matter what he'd been doing that night. What mattered were the lies that had fallen so effortlessly out of his mouth during the weeks they'd been together.

"You're a terrific liar," she said, unable to help the bitterness that crept into her tone.

"You might think so, but you don't realize how difficult it was for me. I hated each and every lie I told you. There's no question that initially I used you to my advantage. But, Julie, it didn't take me long to realize I was falling in love with you. I don't want to take my things and go home. My home is here with you and I will spend the rest of my life trying to make up for all the hurt I've done to you."

Was it possible for him to manufacture the love that shone from his beautiful eyes? Everything was out in the open now; what possible reason would he have to lie about loving her?

Her heart began to beat at a quickened pace. He was who she wanted in her life. Despite their crazy path so far, she believed he loved her. And she loved him.

She might never fully understand why he'd made the choices he had on that night. He was a good man. He could have run right past her car and left her unconscious. It might have been hours before anyone had found her.

He could have dumped her off at her home and exited her life immediately, but he'd seen the remnants of the physical fight she'd had with Casey and had stayed because he'd thought Julie might be in trouble.

Most men would have walked away, unwilling to become embroiled in a stranger's drama, but Nick had stayed. To her surprise, the light of forgiveness filled her heart.

"You'll make it up to me for the rest of your life?" she finally said.

"Just give me the chance, Julie. Give us a chance." He gazed at her intently, as if holding his breath for her reply.

"When are you going to put a ring on my finger?"

A burst of excited laughter escaped him and he jumped up off the sofa. "Today... tomorrow...right now!" he exclaimed as he walked over and pulled her up from the chair and into his arms. "And I'm intending a very short engagement," he said before his lips captured hers in a kiss that nearly took her breath away.

When the kiss finally ended, he placed his hands on either side of her face and stared deeply into her eyes. "Julie, I swear to you I'm the man you dreamed of when you thought of love and marriage. I'm going to be the best husband any woman would ever want."

"And I'm going to be the best wife," she replied. Her heart expanded with happiness. "I think maybe it was fate that brought us together. I was so lonely and ready for love in my life."

He nodded. "And now there's going to be two less lonely people in the world."

"If you start singing that song, I'll never forgive you. Nobody does Air Supply better than Air Supply," she replied.

He laughed and then lowered his head to kiss her once again. This one tasted of his love, of his sweet longing for her. It tasted of the promise of forever.

He raised his head and smiled at her. "I love you, Julie Peterson."

"And I love you, Nick Simon," she replied.

"I can't wait to make you Julie Simon. Maybe we should just elope."

It was her turn to laugh. "My mother would hate you forever if you took away her opportunity to be mother of the bride at a traditional wedding."

"I certainly don't want to start out with the wrath of George and Lynetta focused on me," he said.

"There's no reason why we can't plan a fairly quick wedding."

"Can we enjoy a little honeymoon in your bedroom before the wedding?" His gaze was light and teasing, but with a fiery hunger that instantly lit one in her.

She twirled out of his embrace and ran for the stairs. "Last one up has to cook dinner," she cried over her shoulder.

His laughter chased her up the stairs where they would make love and plan a wedding and plan a future together filled with children and laughter and love.

Epilogue

"Hold them," Nick yelled to the defense. Thank goodness this was a practice and not a real game. The defense still left a lot to be desired. As the play ended, he motioned the teenagers in.

While he waited for them all to gather around, he shot a glance at the bleachers where Julie sat with several of the kids' parents.

As he gave the boys his usual pep talk, his mind drifted over the events of the past two weeks. They had definitely been eventful.

He'd put his house up for sale as he and Julie had decided to live in her place. They'd also been busy making wedding plans. She now sported a pretty diamond engagement ring, pleasing not only her but Lynetta, as well.

He still checked the news every day, hoping not to see any of the names that had been on a hit list of sorts. But that time of his life seemed distant and alien to him now.

As the sweaty boys headed in to the locker rooms, he waved to Julie and followed them. He was thrilled that she was taking an interest in the team and had sworn she would be at all the games.

She'd told her parents she would continue to work part-time at the store until classes began at the community college where she was enrolled. She was taking action on achieving the dream of becoming a nurse.

Casey had been held over for trial and while Julie and the rest of Casey's family were sad at the choices Casey had made, they'd also agreed that she had to face whatever consequences the court handed down.

Once he saw that all the boys were gone from the locker room, he headed toward the bleachers where she was the last one remaining. He couldn't help the way his heart lifted as he approached Julie.

With each day that passed, he only loved her more. She was his heart, his soul, and each day with her was a gift. And the amazing part was that he knew she felt the same way about him.

"Hey, Coach," she said as she stood from the bleacher seat.

"Hey, gorgeous," he replied. "You know what I've always wanted to do?"

"What's that?" Her eyes sparkled with happiness.

"I've always wanted to kiss the woman I'm going to marry on the fifty-yard line."

Her grin was infectious. "Then what are you waiting for?"

He grabbed her hand and together they ran across the neatly manicured grass of the field.

Together...forever...the warmth of love embraced him. It was the way they would run to their future...together and with love.

HE'D SUSPECTED ALL along that when the time to act came, Nick Simon would falter. That was why he had done Brian McDowell. That scumbag had deserved a painful death. A bullet to the head had been too easy.

He'd wanted Brian's death to be slow and painful, which was why he'd brought the large knife with him. It had been so easy. The large flower pot had been a handy tool to throw at the sliding-glass door.

Knowing the noise would rouse Brian out of bed, he'd simply waited in the shadows.

When Brian had stumbled toward the shattered glass, he'd attacked.

Brian had squealed like a pig as he'd driven his knife in him over and over again. God, what a high it had been. His adrenaline had pumped hotter, faster, through his body than he could ever remember. It had been such a rush, like having sex, only better.

He didn't even mind the thick, coppery scent of blood or the ultimate odor of death that wafted in the air when he'd finished. He'd remained seated on the floor next to the body for several long moments.

He'd liked it. He'd liked it so much he was going to do it again. There were a lot of bad people in the world that the justice system had allowed to walk scot-free. He even had a list of the next five men to start with. He'd be patient and he could be careful.

It was time somebody cleaned up the trash on the streets. He wondered how long, how many bodies, it would take before the cops realized the *V* carved into the dead men's foreheads stood for vengeance.

Oh, yes, he couldn't wait to strike again.

* * * * *